EXPLORER ACADEMY

THE NEBULA SECRET

TRUDI TRUEIT

UNDER THE *Stars*

NATIONAL GEOGRAPHIC

FOR WILLIAM, WHO MAKES THE ADVENTURE WORTH TAKING —T.T.

Since 1888, the National Geographic Society has funded more than 12,000 research, exploration, and preservation projects around the world. The Society receives funds from National Geographic Partners, LLC, funded in part by your purchase. A portion of the proceeds from this book supports this vital work. To learn more, visit natgeo.com/info.

For more information, visit nationalgeographic.com, call 1-800-647-5463, or write to the following address:

National Geographic Partners
1145 17th Street N.W.
Washington, D.C. 20036-4688 U.S.A.

Visit us online at nationalgeographic.com/books

For librarians and teachers: ngchildrensbooks.org

More for kids from National Geographic: natgeokids.com

For information about special discounts for bulk purchases, please contact National Geographic Books Special Sales: specialsales@natgeo.com

For rights or permissions inquiries, please contact National Geographic Books Subsidiary Rights: bookrights@natgeo.com

Designed by Eva Absher-Schantz

Library of Congress Cataloging-in-Publication Data

Names: Trueit, Trudi Strain, author.
Title: Explorer Academy/by Trudi Trueit.
Description: Washington, DC : National Geographic Kids, [2018] | Series: Explorer Academy ; [1] | Summary: Twelve-year-old Cruz Coronado leaves his home in Hawaii to study and travel with other young people invited to attend the elite Explorer Academy in Washington, D.C.
Identifiers: LCCN 2017050032 (print) | LCCN 2017058969 (ebook) | ISBN 9781426331619 (e-book) | ISBN 9781426331596 (hardcover) | ISBN 9781426331602 (hardcover)
Subjects: | CYAC: Explorers--Fiction. | Private schools--Fiction. | Schools--Fiction. | Washington (D.C.)--Fiction. | Mystery and detective stories.
Classification: LCC PZ7.T78124 (ebook) | LCC PZ7.T78124 Exp 2018 (print) |DDC [Fic]--dc23
LC record available at https://lccn.loc.gov/2017050032

Printed in the United States of America
18/WOR/1

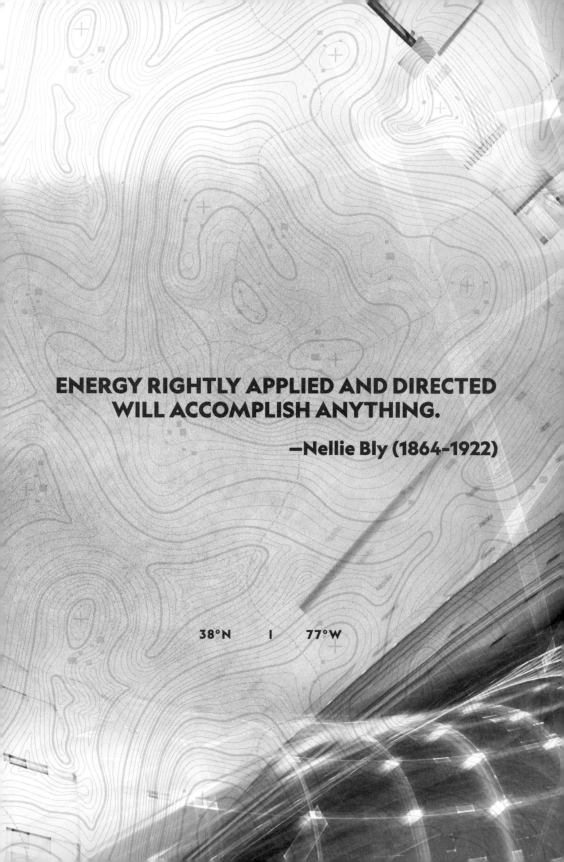

ENERGY RIGHTLY APPLIED AND DIRECTED
WILL ACCOMPLISH ANYTHING.

—Nellie Bly (1864–1922)

38°N | 77°W

1

HANALEI BAY, KAUAI, HAWAII, U.S.A.

PACIFIC OCEAN

HAWAII

O'AHU   MOLOKA'I

KAUA'I   MAUI

LĀNA'I

NI'IHAU   KAHO'OLAWE

PACIFIC OCEAN   HAWAI'I

"CRUZ!"

His name floated easily to him across the water. Cruz turned to see his dad waving him in from the beach. It couldn't be time to go already, could it? Knee-deep in the warm surf, Cruz raised an arm. He spread his fingers to ask—beg—for five more minutes. "Please," he whispered into the evening breeze.

In about three hours, he would be leaving for Explorer Academy. It was a long way from Kauai to Washington, D.C.—4,882 miles, to be exact. And Cruz was scared. What if he didn't make any friends? What if he couldn't handle the training? What if he disappointed his family, his friends, his teachers, and everybody who expected him to be something even *he* wasn't sure he could be?

His father was giving him the thumbs-up.

Yes!

Pushing the what-ifs from his mind, Cruz faced the tangerine sunset of Hanalei Bay. He would think about everything else later. He slid his belly onto the surfboard and began windmilling his arms through the tepid teal waters as he'd done thousands of times. He'd been surfing for as long as he could remember. His dad teased him that he spent more time in the water than out of it, which was probably true. Cruz loved the sweeping motion of the waves. Water was constant and dependable. Comforting.

Approaching the break, Cruz grasped the sides of his surfboard. He pushed the nose underwater in a smooth duck dive and the swell passed over him. Surfacing, he paddled out a bit farther and cut a 45-degree turn that put him parallel to the beach. Lining himself up with the end of the long pier, he sat up and straddled his board, legs dangling. He liked the take-off zone. It was "the calm before the ride," as Lani liked to say. Bobbing like this, he could think about anything or nothing. The choice was up to him. On his last day at home, Cruz didn't want to think. He wanted to feel. He wanted to feel every sensation. And remember.

To his left, beyond the crescent-shaped inlet, rose the emerald peaks of the mountains on the northern shore. In the fading light, it was easy to pick out the white waterfalls cascading down the creases of the hills. Cruz spotted his dad walking through the parking lot— geez, sailboats 20 miles offshore could probably see that crazy-bright yellow-and-blue-zigzag shirt. His father would be headed back up to the Goofy Foot, their surf shop, to close for the night. Cruz glanced right, into the deep orange sunset. It was as if the glowing orb had rolled out a carpet of light across the ocean for him, just to say good-bye. He was sure going to miss this place.

"You don't have to go, you know," Lani had said last spring when he'd told her he'd been accepted into the Academy. Her words stung. Lani was his best friend—the one who always found the silver lining. Not that he blamed her. They had both applied to the school, yet only Cruz had been accepted. It had come as a shock. He had thought Lani surely would have been chosen over him—she was so much smarter and more creative. But then the certified letter had arrived. For *him*. It was impressive, with its fancy parchment paper and shiny gold seal.

Dear Cruz Coronado,

EXPLORER ACADEMY

Congratulations! The Society is pleased to extend to you this invitation of admittance to our elite Explorer Academy. Upon acceptance, you will be inducted into the next class of young explorers and given the rare privilege of learning firsthand from a faculty of the world's most renowned scientists, explorers, conservationists, photographers, and journalists as you travel to historic and majestic locations around the globe. We select only those candidates of the highest caliber for this prestigious honor.

We ardently await your response.

Cordially,

Regina M. Hightower, Ph.D.

Explorer Academy President

Cruz's aunt, Marisol, who taught anthropology at the Academy, said they only accepted 25 or so students per class from around the world. It *was* quite an achievement to be admitted. Still, Cruz wondered, had he earned it? His aunt had likely pulled a few strings to get him in. Or it could have been offered out of guilt. Cruz's mom also once worked at the Society—she had been a neuroscientist with the Synthesis, its scientific arm. Seven years ago, there was a bad accident in her lab. It had taken her life. Another Synthesis scientist, Dr. Elistair Fallowfeld, had also died in the tragedy. That's all anyone would tell Cruz and his family. That, and his mother had been in the wrong place at the wrong time. Cruz hated that saying. Isn't everyone who accidentally dies in the wrong place at the wrong time?

"I thought the plan was for us to go to the Academy *together*," Lani had said to Cruz.

"Yeah, but Aunt Marisol thinks—"

"Of course your aunt wants you to go now. She's going to be there. What do *you* think?"

Cruz knew Lani had wanted him to say he would ask the school to let him wait a year. That would give Lani another chance to apply. He wasn't sure that was a good idea. Cruz was afraid if he didn't go this year they'd never invite him again. There was something else, too. A feeling. No, it was more than a feeling. He couldn't explain it—he only knew he had to obey. "I think ..." His breath had caught. "I think I want to go now."

Lani had thrown her hands up. "That's it, then. Fine. Go."

"Don't be mad. We'll still be able to see each other whenever we want, even when I go aboard *Orion*."

She'd raised a suspicious eyebrow. "Right. Like you're really gonna call me from the explorers' ship halfway around the world."

"Why not? I'll have Mell."

"They're letting you take your MAV?"

Mell was Cruz's honeybee drone, a micro air vehicle (MAV) no bigger than his thumb. It was a gift from his dad last year after Cruz had sprained his knee, so that he would still be able to "see the surf, even if he couldn't feel it." Turned out, he'd only missed a few days of surfing.

"Uh-huh." Cruz had given her a smirk. "See, it won't be so bad. I can give you the scoop on what it's like so when you get in next year you'll be set. All we have to do is pretend you're in your room and I'm in mine, instead of—"

"Half a world away," she'd said wistfully, yet she had been twisting her hair—a sign of surrender.

"Come on, Lani," he had pleaded. "I need your support."

"Okay, okay, but you'd better stay in touch or so help me I will track you down all the way to the North Pole, if I have to."

She wasn't kidding. If Cruz had learned anything it was that when Leilani Kealoha said she would do something, she meant it.

"Absolutely," he'd said. "Easy as Dad's guava pie."

She had folded her arms. "You know I hate pie."

Girls.

There! Cruz spotted his wave. Dropping his chest, he flattened himself against the board. As the swell rolled in behind him, Cruz turned for shore and paddled hard. His strokes were strong and deliberate. Timing was key. Pop up too early and he'd miss the crest. Go too late and he'd wipe out. Cruz could feel the surge growing behind him.

Almost time. Just . . . a few . . . more . . . seconds . . .

When he felt the tail of his board begin to lift, Cruz arched his back, pushed off with his hands, and planted his feet under him—right foot in front and left foot in back, in goofy foot position. Most right-handed people surf with their left foot in front, but not Cruz. Slowly, he lifted himself into a low crouch. The moment the wave broke under him, he let go of the board and rose, arms out for balance. Cruz felt the familiar smooth glide of success. He'd hit the crest perfectly!

"Woo-hoo!" he yelled, angling the board inward. Mist sprayed his face as he made a sweeping S pattern through the curl of water. Cruz shifted his weight, skimming left, then right, then left again to ride the swirl as fast and as far as he could. Surfing made him feel powerful. Free. Invincible! If only the feeling lasted longer than a TV commercial. Cruz rode the wave inland until it dissipated into foam. Reaching for the Velcro strap on his ankle that tethered him to his board, his hand hesitated. It hadn't been five minutes, had it?

Maybe one more run . . .

Charging back into the foam, Cruz tossed his board into the water, hopped on, and paddled out past the break. As before, he scooted upright to straddle his board. Cruz was lifting his left foot

to double-check the ankle strap of the leash when he felt a tug on his right heel. It wasn't a swish, like a fish or turtle passing. It was a good pull. And it could mean only one thing: shark! Cruz tried to slide to the left side of his board, away from the shark, but it had a firm hold on his ankle. He was being dragged down, away from the surface.

Don't panic! KICK!

Cruz clung to his surfboard, the only thing that would keep him afloat, and kicked with all his might. If he could manage to turn around, he could use the board to bop the shark on the nose and break loose. As he struggled, a million thoughts raced through his head.

Stupid! Sharks feed at dusk. You should have gone in when Dad called. You're not supposed to drown. Stupid!

He was swallowing water. He couldn't breathe.

No. No! NO!

The words pounded in rhythm to his heart.

He would not die this way.

With his lungs burning and his energy waning, Cruz twisted his body in one last effort to strike a blow. He lashed out and his fist hit something smooth and hard. Bubbles swarmed around him. He saw a yellow snake. No! A tube. This was no shark. It was a person! His thrashing had knocked the air hose loose from the diver's tank. Cruz felt a sharp pain in his ankle and then, suddenly, he was free! Through the bubbles, he caught sight of a pair of fanning fins. The diver was moving away.

Cruz stroked for the surface, his chest on the verge of exploding. He pushed his arms up through the water, up and out, up and out. He kept his feet moving, kicking, kicking, until finally he breached the surface. Cruz gulped as much air as his lungs could handle. Treading, he spun around, his eyes darting from the pier to the beach to the horizon and back. He did several circles, but didn't see anyone nearby.

Take it easy. You're okay. He's gone. You're okay.

Cruz flung his arm behind him, groping for his surfboard, still tied to his leg. He tried to slide it under his body but was shaking so much it took him a few tries to do what usually came naturally. Clutching his board and looking over his shoulder, he rode the tide in until he scraped bottom. Still gasping, Cruz rolled off the board and onto the wet sand. Never had he been so happy to be back on land! He lay on his back for several minutes, feeling himself breathe. His hands tingled, his throat was raw, and his right ankle throbbed. But he was alive.

As Cruz stared up at the deep violet sky, at the first winking stars of night, one word kept scrolling through his brain: *Why?*

2

"THAT must have been some tsunami," said his dad, locking the door of the surf shop behind Cruz.

"Huh?"

"You look a bit dazed, son."

"I'm okay."

"You cut your leg."

"I did?" Cruz glanced down to see a red line of blood dripping from a gash on his right ankle. "I . . . I guess I snagged it on some coral."

His dad led him to the bathroom in the back of the store. He cleaned the wound. "It's a good cut, but it doesn't look like it needs stitches. I think you'll live."

His dad's words, meant to be soothing, sent a shudder through Cruz. He *was* lucky to be alive. Maybe Cruz should tell his dad what had really happened. If he did, though, his father might change his mind about the Academy. Dad was already on the fence as it was. At first, he hadn't wanted Cruz to go to the school. He'd said Cruz was too young and it was too far from home and the expeditions were too dangerous, but they both knew there was only one reason behind his objection—and it had nothing to do with age, distance, or risk.

After Cruz's mother died, his father had moved them back to Kauai, where he had grown up. Starting over wasn't easy, but they had managed. Cruz's dad opened the Goofy Foot surf shop. Cruz enrolled in a new school and made friends. They found things to do to keep busy on the weekends. They surfed every great and not-so-great beach on the island. They hiked dozens of trails, from Sleeping Giant in the east to Waipoʻo Falls in the west. They even took a rock climbing class. In time, Cruz and his father had begun to heal. Things were stable now—not perfect but no longer raw and painful. Like the beach at low tide, life had a steady and sure rhythm to it. Now Cruz wanted to return to the place where their family had been torn apart, to possibly open the wounds all over again.

"I'm not sure I understand." His dad had stared at him in wonder. "After all that's happened, why would you want to go back *there*?"

"I want to go *everywhere*, Dad. I want to be an explorer."

"You were so young. How could you remember...?"

That much was true. Cruz was five when his mother died. Maybe if he could recall more about their life before this one he wouldn't feel such an urge to go. He'd be satisfied. Or terrified.

"Cruz?" His father was nudging him back to the present.

"Yeah?"

"I said, you're not hurt anywhere else, are you? Did you hit your head?"

"No."

"Why don't you go on up? I'll finish here. By the way, Lani came by."

"She did?" Cruz wondered why she hadn't come down to the beach.

"She left something for you. One sec." His dad went to the front of the store and returned with a small turquoise gift bag.

Fishing through layers of tissue paper, Cruz took out a card and a white, square box. He opened the card.

> *Now you can control Mell anywhere,*
> *anytime. Well, not anywhere.*
> *Your range is about 4,000 feet.*
> *Aloha, Lani*
> *P.S. I told you I could do it!*

Cruz lifted the lid off the box. Sitting on a cushion of cotton was a tiny pin in the shape of a honeycomb. He let out a laugh. Leave it to Lani to not only take him up on a dare but to come through. "She did it!"

His dad tilted his head. "What is it?"

"It's to communicate with Mell," said Cruz, holding the pin up between his thumb and index finger. "Lani made a voice-command remote so I don't have to use the controller or my phone. I'm pretty sure her mom helped her with it, but still..."

"She's a smart one, that Leilani," said his dad.

Forgetting about his ankle, Cruz zipped up the back stairs to their apartment above the store. He raced to his bedroom and attached the pin to his T-shirt. "Mell, turn on," he said loudly and clearly.

The tiny carbon-fiber bee sitting on his shelf flashed its eyes from black to gold. The remote worked!

"Mell, come to me," said Cruz. Within seconds the computer honey-bee, only slightly larger than a real bee, hovered inches from his nose. "Mell, sit on my shoulder," he said. The bee obeyed. Wild!

Cruz fired up his computer. The second Lani answered the video call, he burst out, "Mell, speak and wave to Lani on the computer."

Buzzing, Mell wagged an antenna.

Lani laughed and waved back. "I'm just glad it works."

"It's perfect." Admiration dripped from his words.

"Make sure you give it clear commands, okay?"

"I will. Thanks, Lani."

"You're welcome." She beamed.

"Hey, how come you didn't come down to the beach?" asked Cruz.

"I don't know." Her smile melted. "I figured you'd want to be alone. Last day and all."

"You should have." He checked behind him to make sure his dad hadn't come up. "You are *not* going to believe what happened to me!"

"What?"

"Someone tried to drown me!"

She snorted. "Sure they did."

"I'm not kidding," he said. "They grabbed my leg and tried to drag me underwater..."

"I'll bet it was one of the lifeguards pulling a prank. Who's that kid that's always throwing grapes at us when we go by? Manu or Mano Somebody—"

"It wasn't a lifeguard, Lani. It was someone in scuba gear: fins, mask, tank—the works. I'm tellin' you, he tried to kill me and he almost did."

Her expression changed when she realized he was not joking. "Who would want to hurt you?"

"I don't know."

"Are you okay?"

He turned his ankle. It had stopped throbbing. "Yeah."

"Your dad must have freaked out when you told him."

"I didn't exactly—"

"Told me what?"

Cruz spun. "Uh ... hi, Dad. She means about the coral." He turned back to Lani. "Nah, he's seen me do much worse than that!" Cruz made an O shape with his mouth to signal to her he didn't want his dad to know any more.

She got the message. "Have a good trip, Cruz. Be *safe*, okay?"

"I will."

"Because if you don't watch your step, I'll track you down all the way—"

"To the North Pole—I know." Cruz touched the honeycomb pin. "Thanks again."

"Aloha," she said, her voice cracking.

"Aloha."

His screen went dark.

Cruz's dad was sitting on the edge of the bed, a cream-colored envelope in his hand.

"Is that for me?" prompted Cruz.

His father tapped the envelope against his knee. "Yes."

Another 30 seconds passed.

"You ... uh ... planning on handing it over this year?" teased Cruz. He guessed it must have money in it. His dad always had a hard time parting with dollars.

"That's a good question." His dad rubbed his forehead. "Sorry. I'm not quite sure how to do this."

Cruz sat up. Maybe it wasn't cash, after all.

"I've practiced it a thousand times," said his father, "and now I can't seem to ... I guess I should say it and be done with it, right?"

"That's what you always tell me."

"Okay. Here goes. Straight out. Just gonna say it."

"*Daaaad.*"

"It's a letter from your mother."

Cruz jumped and Mell fell off his shoulder. The bee quickly recovered and circled up to land on him again. "Mell, turn off," ordered Cruz, catching the robotic insect. He placed it on his desk. "It's from ... Mom? I don't get it. How ...?"

"We never talked about her projects," explained his dad, "but I knew her work at the Synthesis was ... difficult. Even dangerous. I made her a promise that if anything ever happened I would give this letter to you on your thirteenth birthday."

"But I won't be thirteen until—"

"November twenty-ninth, I know," he said, "but you'll be at the Academy then and it doesn't seem right to make you wait until winter break ... I *did* promise, but ..." He stood up. "It's bad timing now, isn't it? You're leaving in a couple of hours. What was I thinking? We should do this later—"

"No!" Cruz leaped up. Was his dad kidding? Cruz had no intention of waiting even one more minute for a letter from his mother. "It's okay, Dad," he said gently, holding out his hand. "I can handle it."

His dad placed the envelope in Cruz's outstretched palm, his body instantly relaxing, as if he was glad to finally be rid of the burden. He saw Cruz's open suitcase on the bed. "You all packed?"

"Pretty much."

"Are you sure you want to take that?" He nodded to the silver metal dome the size of a small snow globe tucked into the corner of the suitcase.

"Why not?"

"It's more delicate than it looks. It could break on the flight. Or get confiscated if the authorities think it's a weapon."

His dad was right, of course. He couldn't risk losing his most prized possession. Cruz's shoulders sagged. "I'll leave it."

"Don't worry, it'll be safe here." Standing, his father headed for the door. "You should take a catnap if you can, son. It's a long flight."

"Dad?" Cruz held up the letter. "Don't you want to ...?"

"No. It's for you. I'll wake you in an hour." He left, softly shutting the door behind him.

Cruz stared at the parchment envelope. Turned it over a few times. There was no writing on either side, not even his name. What was he waiting for? Cruz slid his index finger under the flap. It easily popped up.

His pulse quickening, he took out a thin, folded page made from the same creamy paper as the envelope. Gently, Cruz unfolded it. The black ink was a little faded, the slanted handwriting like delicate lace:

My dearest Cruz,

If you are reading this, it means I am not with you, and for that I am truly and deeply sorry. Bringing you into the world and watching you grow has been my greatest joy. I would love nothing more than to be there in person to give you a birthday hug, but sadly, this letter will have to do. My wish for you this year, and for all the years to come, is a life filled with discovery, passion, contribution, friendship, kindness, peace, and love. These are the things that give our lives meaning, whether we live for a day or a century. Happy 13th birthday. Never forget, you are an extraordinary being. Most important, never forget I love you.

Mom

Sometimes Cruz missed his mother so much it hurt. Physically hurt. Like when you have the flu and ache from your bones out. Cruz took the metal dome from his suitcase. It felt cold. Placing it on his nightstand, he tapped the side. Instantly, a three-dimensional holographic video recording of his mother appeared a few inches above its silver projector base. Cruz was in the video, too. He was about three years old. They were at the beach. He didn't know where, but it must have been chilly, because they were both bundled up. Cruz was wearing a yellow raincoat with ducks around the hem and a matching hat. In his yellow galoshes, he was intently digging a trench around himself with a red plastic shovel. Watching him create his own little island in the sand and knowing she'd have to rescue him when he finished, his mother couldn't resist giggling. Her long blond hair billowed in the brisk wind like a festival of kites.

"Look at him dig, Marco," his mom said to his dad, who was behind the camera. "Our budding archaeologist."

"And you were so hoping he'd go into neurobiology," teased his dad.

"He can do both," she said, turning to her child. "You can do anything you set your mind to, Cruzer."

"Mama, help!" It was strange, watching his tiny younger self hold out his little arms to her.

Bending to scoop him up, her gray-blue eyes crinkled with happiness. The scene flickered, then faded into nothing with the two of them locked in a tight hug.

Seeing his mother usually comforted Cruz, but not this time. Not tonight.

Tonight, he hurt.

3

WEST
VIRGINIA

MARYLAND

VIRGINIA

DELAWARE

ATLANTIC
OCEAN

WASHINGTON,
D.C., U.S.A.

AS THE plane banked left and the spire of the

Washington Monument appeared in his window, Cruz nearly let out
a cheer. He'd made it! After 13 hours (including stops in Seattle and
Detroit), a soggy veggie burger, a broken seat-back TV, and a howling
Chihuahua three rows back, he was finally about to touch down in
the nation's capital.

His left leg was asleep and his right ankle itched. *Oops!* He'd promised his dad he would change the bandage on his cut *before* he got to
Washington, D.C. Technically, he still had about five minutes to make
good on that vow. Quickly, Cruz slid down his sock and pulled off the
old bandage. Where last night there had been a long red gash, there
was now a thin pink line. Maybe the wound hadn't been as deep as
his dad had thought. Cruz balled up the bandage and stuffed it in his
pocket. Once the plane touched down at Reagan National Airport,
Cruz sent his dad a quick text to tell him he'd arrived.

Inside the terminal, Cruz spotted his aunt right away. She was
wearing a bright pink suit and a scarf with pink flamingos held in
place by a giant enamel flamingo pin. Didn't it figure? Aunt Marisol
had the same bold taste in clothing as Cruz's dad. Athletic yet graceful,
his aunt also had the same off-center smile and bright white teeth as
his dad. Her thick, dark hair was pulled into a loose bun. Pink high heels
were striding toward him. Within seconds, a pair of arms were around

him and all he could see was a ton of blurry pink birds. Cruz didn't mind. He'd missed her, too. He squeezed back.

His aunt pulled away to inspect him. "You must have grown a foot since spring."

"Three-quarters of an inch."

"Then it must be all this hair." She tugged on a lock above his ear that was the same dark chocolate shade as her own. "Doesn't that brother of mine ever take you for a haircut?"

Cruz rolled his eyes. "Aunt Marisol."

"Did you get my postcard from Italy?"

"Uh-huh."

"And?"

"You're going to have to give me harder stuff to decode." When she gave him a disbelieving smirk, he said, "Your message said you were excited for me to come and that you'd meet my plane … oh, and to look for the pink birds." Cruz eyed her outfit. "You weren't kidding, were you?"

"Good work. Tell me how you did it?" she asked. He knew finding out how he'd gone about deciphering her message was her favorite part of their game.

"Let's see; there was a picture of a lion statue on the front of the postcard and the postmark was from Narni, Italy, so it was pretty obvious you were referring to your favorite series, the Chronicles of Narnia," said Cruz. "Once I knew that, I had to figure out which book of the seven you'd chosen for a cipher. At first, I thought it was *The Lion, the Witch and the Wardrobe* 'cause of the lion statue, but *The Magician's Nephew* seemed a better choice, since I am your nephew and you wouldn't want to make it *too* easy for me. Next, it was a matter of figuring out which page to use as the cipher. On the jacket flap I read that C. S. Lewis's birthday is November twenty-ninth, which is also my birthday. I knew that had to be more than a coincidence. I flipped to page eleven and started with the twenty-ninth word and ta-da— message decoded."

"Nicely done, Special Agent Cruz," said his aunt. "Narnia was your mom's favorite series, too. She must have read *The Lion, the Witch and the Wardrobe* a hundred times. The two of us would use it to write coded notes to each other back in our Academy days when we were supposed to be listening to our teachers—not that you'd dare do anything like that in one of *my* anthropology classes, right?"

"Never." He gave her a Cheshire grin.

"Oh, I nearly forgot! I brought someone from the Academy with me." Aunt Marisol motioned toward a boy about Cruz's age standing near her. He was wearing a Toronto Blue Jays baseball cap, oval-shaped lime green glasses, a blue T-shirt, and jeans. "This is Emmett Lu, one of your roommates. Emmett, this is my nephew, Cruz."

"Hi!" said Cruz, a little too enthusiastically.

"Hey." Emmett nodded. "Dr. Coronado was telling me about the bee drone you built. Did you bring it?"

"Yep," said Cruz, lifting his backpack, "but I...I...didn't build Mell. I only programmed it. Although I did upgrade the camera from a thirty to three hundred millimeter, ten-X cinema zoom."

"Cool! I can't wait to see it in action."

"I'll fly it for you when we get to the Academy."

"I had a feeling the two of you might hit it off," said Aunt Marisol, tapping at her phone. "We're also picking up your other roommate... He's from New Zealand... Uh-oh—looks like his flight is coming in early from New York. Why don't I run down and get him while the two of you grab your suitcase?" She walked backward, pink heels click-clacking against the shiny floor. "I'll meet you at that grill near the main entrance. Emmett, you know the one, right? Good. If you're hungry, get something to eat because the dining hall at the Academy will be closed." They watched her rush off, the ends of her long flamingo scarf becoming wings.

They went to baggage claim to pick up Cruz's suitcase, then headed up to the café. The smell of cooking food set Cruz's stomach rumbling. They stood in line and Cruz ordered a grilled cheese sandwich and a cup of tomato soup. He offered to buy something for Emmett, too.

"Thanks, but I'm fine," said Emmett. He took off his cap, pushed his black hair up off his forehead, and straightened his green glasses. "I had thirds at dinner an hour ago."

"Dinner?" Cruz glanced at the airplane-shaped clock above the cash register. It read three minutes after 7 p.m. "This is lunch for me. It's only one o'clock back in Kauai."

"That's right, you've lost time," said Emmett.

"Six hours of my life—gone, poof! It doesn't seem fair, does it? We should build a time machine for people who fly so they can get back some of their lost time."

Emmett started to laugh, then paused. "You know, that *would* be a cool project. We'd win the North Star, for sure."

Cruz knew about the North Star award. It was given to the new explorer who showed the most promise at the end of his or her first year.

"We could be the first co-winners in school history," said Emmett.

"Sounds good to me," said Cruz, tasting his tomato soup. It was hot and a little spicy. Perfect!

"My dad won the North Star when he was at the Academy." Emmett slid his triangular, sky blue frames up his nose.

"No pressure there, huh?" Cruz did a double take. "Hey! Weren't your glasses green a minute ago? And round?"

"They're emoto- glasses. They change color and shape based on my emotions."

"Now *that* is cool. I've never seen anything like it."

"You won't. I made them."

"You *made* them?"

"It's a simple program, really. You inject a few neurotransmitter nano-processors into the bloodstream to target the brain and lock on to key neurons, which then relay levels of dopamine, serotonin, and noradrena-line to the microprocessor in the glasses, which then selects the prepro-grammed corresponding color in the visible spectrum in real time. Easy!"

Cruz dropped his spoon.

"The tricky part," continued Emmett, "was creating a lightweight composite that wasn't too thermally sensitive. The last thing you want when you get mad is for your glasses to melt into a puddle on the floor. That took me a few tries. Okay, fifty-seven tries."

Cruz let out a low whistle. He wouldn't have kept at it for that long.

"Once I had that," said Emmett, "it was only a matter of designing the receptacle frames and producing them on my 4-D printer."

"4-D?" Cruz knew 3-D meant height, width, and depth. "What's the fourth D?"

"Time, of course. That's not my theory. That's Einstein's. Well, tech-nically, Einstein's professor's theory, but Einstein made it famous." He grinned. "That's why your time travel idea isn't as out there as you might think. Right now, I'm working on fabric that will transform itself based on the wearer's preferences. Say you want your shirt to go from crew neck to V-neck or from floral to stripes. All you'd have to do is think about what you wanted and the fabric would comply."

"Could you really do that?"

"Yes," he answered matter-of-factly. "It is possible. We already have mind-control technology for digital gear, like cameras and computers, so it's not out of the realm of possibility to extend that to ideas, memories, and even dreams. I still have some work to do on Lumagine. That's what I'm calling my fabric—you know, Lu, for my last name, combined with 'imagine.' But I'll get there."

Cruz chuckled. "If I were you, Emmett, I wouldn't worry about losing that award."

"Thanks," Emmett said shyly, his triangular glasses softening at the tips. "We'll see."

Cruz finished his soup and half of the grilled cheese sandwich before sliding the plate toward Emmett. "Sure you're not hungry? I'm full and there's still plenty left."

"If you're not going to eat it…" As Emmett reached for the toasted triangle oozing cheddar, Cruz noticed a gold band on his wrist. It was more than an inch wide yet paper thin, with an opaque white screen that shimmered when it caught the sunlight. This must be something Emmett had invented, he thought. Cruz waited to see if the gold band would change color, too. It didn't.

They talked about other stuff, like their favorite sports (soccer for Emmett, surfing for Cruz), favorite foods (lasagna for Emmett, pizza for Cruz), and their families (neither of them had siblings).

"There's my aunt," Cruz said as Emmett took his last bite.

High heels were click-clacking toward them. Aunt Marisol was pulling a purple suitcase on wheels. "Sorry … we took so long." She was out of breath.

Emmett looked past her. "Where's the Kiwi?"

She pushed aside several strands of hair that had fallen from her bun. "Coming … Bathroom stop … Here we go!" Aunt Marisol flung her arm around a pair of shoulders. "Boys, meet Sailor York."

Cruz and Emmett froze. This was their new roommate?

"Hi," said a slim girl with mocha brown eyes and olive skin. She flipped back a lock of long hazelnut-colored hair. "Good to meet ya."

"H-hi," said Cruz.

Emmett's brow wrinkled. "I didn't think they let boys and girls—"

"They don't," clipped Aunt Marisol. "Minor glitch. We'll sort it out. And the sooner the better. Let's go, everyone."

Cruz and Emmett cleared their table. Everything went into recycle and compost bins. As they trailed Aunt Marisol and Sailor to the exit, Cruz noticed Emmett kept glancing behind them. "Did you forget something?" he asked.

"No." Emmett's glasses had morphed into half-moons the color of raisins. "I was … uh … watching to see if that guy was still around."

The hairs on Cruz's arms stood up. "What guy?"

"He was on your flight, came through the gate right after you. I saw him at baggage claim and again at the café. When we got up to leave, he got up, too, even though he hadn't touched his food. That's what got me wondering—"

Cruz whirled. "Where?"

Emmett's head swiveled. "I … uh … I don't see him anymore … He must have gone the other way."

"What did he look like?"

"He had sunglasses on so it was hard to see his face, but he was wearing a leather jacket, jeans, and black cowboy boots. I think it had snakeskin print on the toes. I'm not sure. It could have been a cow print."

Cruz didn't like the sound of this. First someone tries to drown him, and now he's being followed?

Emmett shrugged. "Guess it was one of those weird coincidences, huh?"

"Guess so," said Cruz, but he wasn't convinced.

If Aunt Marisol's puzzles had taught him anything, it was that coincidence is rare. Things almost always happen for a reason, even if you don't see it. Cruz took another glance behind them. He saw nothing.

TO DISCOVER. TO INNOVATE.

TO PROTECT. Cruz forgot to exhale as his gaze swept over the school's motto, etched in marble above steel doors, a row of white marble columns, and a steep, pointed roof that seemed to tap the sky. He remembered to breathe again only when they reached the summit of the limestone steps.

"That's our room," said Emmett, pointing to a window in the top corner of the building. "Fifth floor, last window on the left."

The inside of the Academy was almost as imposing as the outside. Blinding white marble with tiny black veins running through it covered the walls and floor of the vast lobby. A relief map of the world covered almost an entire wall. Fan-shaped black sconces sent V-shaped rays of light upward, while ornate, black iron lamps topped with trapezoid black-and-white stained glass shades illuminated the simple lines of black leather chairs and sofas. Most of the seats in the spacious room were filled with middle- and high-school-age kids talking or bent over their phones and tablets. Plush black-and-white rugs led to a tall, black granite front desk so shiny Cruz could see his reflection in it. Cruz motioned for Aunt Marisol to go ahead of him with Sailor.

"See you up there," Emmett said to Cruz, heading for the elevator. "Fifth floor. Mount Everest room. FYI, all the dorm rooms are named after natural wonders of the world."

Of course they were! This was Explorer Academy, after all.

While Cruz waited to check in, he studied the rug beneath him. It was woven with Egyptian figures and hieroglyphs. Thanks to Aunt Marisol's cryptographic puzzles, Cruz was familiar with the ancient form of writing. He knew what many of the symbols stood for, like the looped cross, which was the sign for life, and the sun, which represented the passage of time.

Aunt Marisol turned from the desk. "Sailor is all set in one of the *girls'* rooms."

"I'm in the Great Barrier Reef room," giggled Sailor. "Doesn't it just figure? I've come fourteen thousand kilometers away from home only to end up down under all over again."

They laughed.

Sailor picked up her suitcase. "Thanks for everything, Professor Coronado. See ya in class. Sweet as to meet you, Cruz."

"Sweet as what?"

"Just 'sweet as.' It's a Kiwi thing. I know it's a sentence fragment, but..."

Cruz felt himself relax. Maybe making new friends wasn't going to be as hard as he'd imagined. "Sweet as to meet you, too," he said.

"Do you need help getting settled?" his aunt asked as they watched Sailor roll her purple suitcase to the elevator.

"I've got it," said Cruz.

She let out the same satisfied sigh his dad did on Saturdays when he got the last item crossed off his to-do list. "I'm going to head home and check in with your dad. He said you injured your foot surfing." She glanced down. "You okay?"

"Yep. See?" Cruz bounced from one foot to the other. His ankle felt as if it had never been hurt at all.

"Good, so call or text if you need anything." A slow smile warmed her face. "You're going to love the Academy. How many kids your age get to go on an archaeological dig for a lost civilization or help save an endangered species? It's the adventure of a lifetime, you know."

"I know." He was excited, but nervous, too.

She squeezed his shoulder. "See you tomorrow."

"Bye, Aunt Marisol."

A boy a year or two older than Cruz, his leg slung over the arm of a leather chair, nodded toward the pink suit leaving the lobby. "Is that your aunt?"

Cruz pretended not to hear.

"Hey! I'm talkin' to you, surfer dude!"

Cruz glanced down at his Goofy Foot surf shop tee. Hesitant, he tapped his chest.

"Yeah, you." The boy was wearing a red T-shirt that said *I'm Kind of a Big Deal*. "Is Professor Coronado your aunt?"

"Uh … well …" Cruz inched toward the front desk, but the young woman who'd helped Sailor had stepped into the back office.

"Guys, get this," barked Big Deal. "He's Dr. Coronado's nephew."

Four heads spun. "Who?"

Cruz felt his face glow. "I … I …"

Big Deal let out a whistle. "Renshaw, you and all the other newbies might as well kiss the North Star award goodbye right now."

"Not me," spouted a gangly boy sitting nearby. A sunburned nose and cheeks were covered in brown freckles. His hair was cut so short you could see a small mole on the side of his skull. "That award is mine. Dugan Marsh. M-A-R-S-H. Spell it right on the trophy, people."

That got hoots from the younger explorers and snorts from the older ones.

"Thank you for that bold yet premature comment, Mr. Marsh." The desk clerk was back, her shoulders barely clearing the top of the granite desk. The petite woman had bright green eyes and a short crop of hair that reminded Cruz of a sparrow's feathers. A badge reading *Taryn* was pinned on her red turtleneck by her collarbone. "Need I remind you," she said sternly, "that the North Star award is based on many factors, including performance, attitude, and potential? The administration, faculty, and *staff* have input in selecting the winner, and I can assure you that *no one,* not even this young explorer here, will get preferential treatment."

A hush fell over the lobby. All eyes turned to Cruz, who wished he could disappear into the carpet and hide among the Egyptians. This was not how he'd wanted to start things at the Academy. This kind of news was bound to spread faster than head lice at summer camp. Everyone would believe he was here because his aunt had pulled strings. How could he blame them when a part of him believed it, too?

"Also, there's no trophy," said Taryn. "The winner gets their name engraved on the big crystal pyramid in the library."

Cruz felt a hand on his shoulder. "Don't let him get to you," whispered a voice. Turning slightly, Cruz glanced up into friendly eyes that not even a mass of dark curls could hide. "I've heard some of the recruits will try to mess with your head," said the boy, who was a good two inches taller than Cruz. "Some of them can't handle friendly competition."

"I can," said Cruz.

"Then we're going to get along great." The boy stuck out his hand. "Zane Patrick."

"Cruz Coronado." Cruz clasped ebony fingers and they shook. Zane had a strong grip.

"*Rrr-ruff!*" They looked down to see the eager, black button eyes of a West Highland white terrier gazing up at them.

"Hiya, pup!" said Cruz, kneeling.

"That's Hubbard," said Taryn. "He's my dog but he gets spoiled by all the attention from the explorers, so he thinks he owns the place."

Cruz let the Westie give his hand a good sniff before scratching the dog between his ears.

"*Ruff, ruff!*" Hubbard's tail became a fluffy white pendulum of joy.

"Next please." Taryn was calling for Cruz. Standing, he stepped up to the desk.

"I'm Taryn Secliff, your dorm adviser. If you have any questions, problems, concerns, complaints, needs, or wants, you are to come to me. I'm around twenty-four seven, except Saturdays between noon and seven p.m.—that's my afternoon off. During the day, you can usually find me working here at the front desk, and at night you can find me on the fifth floor in the Sahara room, just off the elevator between the girls' and boys' hallways—that's where I live. From there, I hear, see, and know everything that goes on. *Everything.* Got it?"

Translation: Don't do anything stupid, Cruz thought.

"Got it," said Cruz.

"Oh, and please don't feed Hubbard. He had a bit of a weight problem with all of the explorers slipping him food, so now all meals and treats come from me."

"Okay."

"Hold out your left wrist, palm up."

Cruz's heart fluttered. "My ... my ... left ...?"

"Yes, your left arm. And remove your bracelet."

Cruz slid off his elastic Aztec dragon bracelet made from red and green beads—a birthday gift from Aunt Marisol last year. His dad had one, too.

When he held out his wrist, Taryn said what he knew she'd say. "Such an unusual birthmark." She turned his arm to get a better look at the rose-colored, twisted ladder on the inside of his wrist. "It looks like a double helix. Very cool."

He had not expected her to say *that*. For most of his life, he had been teased about the two-inch blemish. He had learned to use wristbands, bracelets, watches, sleeves, and even duct tape to keep it hidden.

Taryn snapped a gold band like Emmett's on him. Over the next 15 seconds, the band slowly tightened, conforming to his arm like a second skin. It was so light he barely felt it. "This is your OS band. It stands for 'Organic Synchronization,' although the explorers just call it the Open Sesame band. It's your passkey. Hold it up to a security cam and it will get you into anyplace explorers are allowed in the complex. It uses the electrical activity of your heart to identify you."

"It's a miniature electrocardiogram machine?"

"Precisely. It also monitors all vital signs, brain function, immune system, growth patterns, physical activity, calorie count, and whether you've brushed your teeth."

"Really?"

"Just kidding about that last one."

Cruz chuckled.

"However, do *not* lose it or you really can kiss the North Star award goodbye. Carelessness is one of Dr. Hightower's pet peeves."

Cruz gave her a solemn nod. "I won't forget."

"A word to the wise?" She cocked an eyebrow. "Don't focus on the award. You'll try too hard. Desperation almost always leads to error."

"Then what should I do?"

"Work a lot. Play a little. Let the rest take care of itself." Taryn handed him a computer about the same size and thickness as a greeting card. It had a black neoprene protective covering. "This is your digital notebook. Use it for all assignments, training sessions, and field notes. It has a keyboard touch screen but also a stylus embedded at the top right corner. The tablet contains your orientation video, class schedule, school rules, and campus map. Review and memorize, please. The dining hall is behind me; head down the hall and you'll see it on your left. Your classroom is inside the library, which is at the end of the corridor past the dining hall. The main entrance to the CAVE is in the basement. Use the staircase at the far end of the lobby."

"CAVE?"

"'Computer Animated Virtual Experience.' It's where you'll do your training missions."

A simulator? As Sailor would say, sweet as!

"Do *not* lose your personal computer," said Taryn. "Like I said, big pet peeve. Orientation is tomorrow at seven a.m. in the library classroom with a full day of classes after that, so while I know it may be tempting to enjoy your freedom—don't. Get your rest. You'll need it. Nobody sleeps through class around here."

Cruz *was* tired. He hadn't slept much on the plane.

"You're in the Mount Everest room," said Taryn. "Take the elevator up to the fifth floor—"

"Thanks, I know the way." He flung his backpack over one shoulder.

"One more word?" She bent her cropped brown head. "Opportunity comes in many forms. It's not how you get it that matters but what you do with it."

Cruz knew what she was getting at, but if the other explorers were convinced he was being favored, nothing he said or did was likely to change their minds. How could he possibly prove to them, and himself, that he belonged here? Giving Hubbard a good-night scratch, Cruz reached for his suitcase.

"Oh, and, Cruz?"

He straightened. "Yes?"

"Welcome to the Academy."

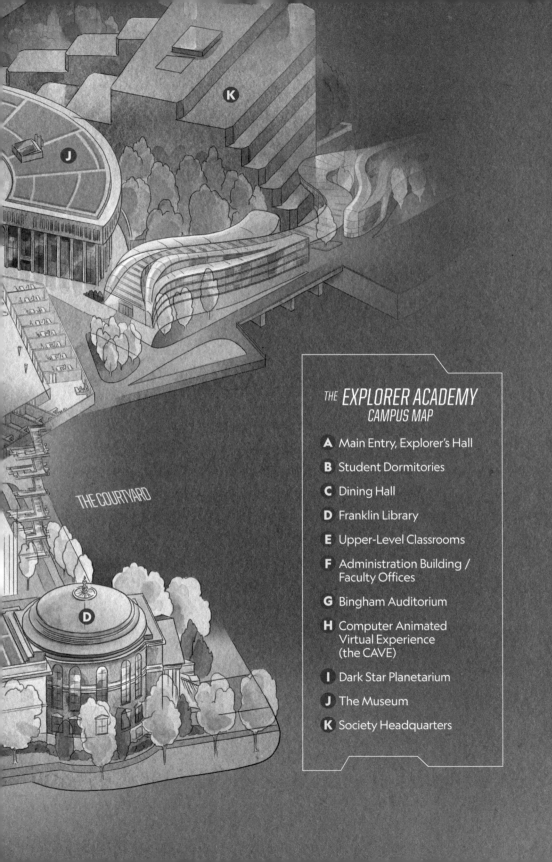

THE COURTYARD

THE **EXPLORER ACADEMY**
CAMPUS MAP

A Main Entry, Explorer's Hall

B Student Dormitories

C Dining Hall

D Franklin Library

E Upper-Level Classrooms

F Administration Building /
Faculty Offices

G Bingham Auditorium

H Computer Animated
Virtual Experience
(the CAVE)

I Dark Star Planetarium

J The Museum

K Society Headquarters

5

EMMETT took a big bite of his Belgian waffle smothered in bananas and whipped cream. "Hey, Cruz, what's wrong? Don't you like your breakfast?"

Cruz glanced down at the velvet blanket of blackberry syrup flowing over a jumble of fresh blackberries, raspberries, and blueberries and down a stack of golden pancakes. Next to the pancakes, steam rose from a fluffy mound of white cheddar cheese scrambled eggs. Two pieces of lightly crisped bacon were tucked in neatly beside the eggs. "I like it fine," said Cruz, turning the gold-rimmed plate. "I was trying to decide whether to eat it or donate it to the art museum."

Emmett laughed, as did the other guys at their table—Zane, Ali Soliman, and Renshaw McKittrick. Zane was from San Francisco; Ali lived in Cairo, Egypt; and Renshaw came from a small town in Scotland called Eckle-Freckle-Something-or-Other. Renshaw and Zane roomed across the hall from Emmett and Cruz in the Victoria Falls room while Ali was next door in Grand Canyon with Dugan Marsh, who was from Santa Fe, New Mexico. "I know everything about the Grand Canyon," Dugan had informed them last night, when everyone had gathered in the fifth-floor lounge for popcorn. "It's two hundred seventy-seven miles long, up to eighteen miles wide, and more than a mile deep."

Cruz noticed that Dugan liked to spout facts, figures, and other bits of trivia. Was he trying to impress? Or intimidate? Given what

Cruz knew about him so far, probably a little of both.

It hadn't taken Cruz long to settle into Everest with Emmett. Their corner room wasn't large, but it had everything they needed: a compact 3-D printer, plenty of closet and drawer space, soft mattresses and pillows, and a private bathroom. The walls were painted an icy blue. On the longest wall hung a large, full-color picture of Mount Everest. Cruz started in for a closer look. "Great photo."

"That's no photo," corrected Emmett. "That's a real-time view of Mount Everest. The web cam is streaming live from one of the base camps."

Cruz shook his head in amazement. This place was full of surprises!

Renshaw was elbowing Cruz. The fair-skinned boy from Scotland had been in the lobby last night when Cruz had checked in and heard the comments from Big Deal. Renshaw tipped his ash blond head toward Cruz's practically untouched breakfast. "Nervous?"

"A little," confessed Cruz. He had tried to eat, but the few bites he could manage of his very berry pancakes were doing a very merry dance in his stomach. Watching Emmett shovel food into his mouth and Zane laugh at something Ali said, he wondered how they could all be so calm. They were all minutes away from starting training at *the* Academy. Weren't they scared, too?

"I know what ya mean," said Renshaw, yawning. "I barely slept last night. I could use a wee kip right now."

"Huh?"

"A nap. Don't ya worry, Cruz. We'll help each other get through. My brother says that's how it's done: Everybody helps everybody else. The teachers encourage that."

"Thanks." That did make him feel better. "So your brother went here?"

"Still does. Jovan's a year ahead of us. He's the top explorer in his class. He won the North Star award last year."

"Wow!"

"Aye, he's great," said Renshaw, squinting the way you do when the sun stings your eyes. "You'd better eat up. You don't want your stomach growling all through orientation, do you?"

"No," snickered Cruz.

Taking a swig of milk, Cruz looked at his daily class schedule one more time. Not that he needed to. He had it memorized. Cruz had six classes: conservation, anthropology (with Aunt Marisol), fitness and survival training, biology, world geography, and journalism. His calendar also showed he had CAVE training. Their time in the simulator would be an extension of their classwork, with the professors taking turns assigning missions. He was also required to take an evening class twice a week on a subject that interested him, such as computer coding, art, or music. Cruz had looked at the list but hadn't yet decided which class to sign up for. Maybe photography or pottery, he thought. Emmett was taking composite materials design, which sounded cool, but Cruz didn't want to intrude. Lani, who had two brothers and two sisters, had told him it was important to give your roommate breathing room.

"Come on, Cruz, we're gawn," said Renshaw.

Cruz was confused until he saw his Scottish friend scoot out of his chair. Renshaw meant they were *going*. Cruz was learning that just because the other explorers spoke English, it didn't necessarily make for easy communication! Tucking his tablet under his arm, Cruz cleared his place. Everything was recyclable, including their leftover food, which went into the compost bin. Turning left out of the dining room, they headed down the wide marble corridor toward the library.

Cruz must have looked worried, because Renshaw bumped his shoulder with his own and said, "My brother says orientation is easy."

"Good to know," said Cruz.

Bounding toward the library entrance, the boys were met by a wiry man with brick red hair and a neatly trimmed beard. "Everybody's so excitable today! Welcome, recruits!" An easy smile revealed gleaming white teeth, his deep voice boomed with friendliness. "Rook," he said, holding out his hand for Cruz to shake. "Everything you see around you is yours, day or night. If there's anything my staff or I can do to assist you in your studies, please be sure to stop by the checkout desk. We are here to help you succeed."

Tipping his head back, Cruz peered around the rotunda. He'd never seen so many books! Five levels of shelves encased the round library. Curved metal staircases led from one level to the next. The ceiling was painted entirely like the night sky, but for a small circular window at the top that let in the morning light.

"It is something, isn't it?" said Dr. Rook, glancing up. "The stars are painted in the same formation they were the very night the Society was founded in 1888."

"Whoa!" Cruz did a slow circle to take it all in.

"What's that, Dr. Rook?" Emmett pointed to a rounded door that broke up the line of shelves on the fifth tier.

"It's *Mr.* Rook," said the librarian. "And *that* is our special collections room. It's where we keep our rare and first-edition books, one-of-a-kind photographs, antique documents, that sort of thing. Access is restricted, though. To get inside, you must be accompanied by myself or my assistant, Dr. Holland. I'm happy to take you anytime, but right now you'd better get to orientation. To get to the classroom, head straight back through reference and world cultures, then veer right at Nellie Bly." Mr. Rook moved past them to welcome more students. "Greetings, new recruits!"

Cruz looked at Emmett. "Who's Nellie Bly?"

"An American explorer," answered a different voice. Cruz turned to find a grinning Sailor York over his shoulder. "Ever heard of Jules Verne's novel *Around the World in Eighty Days*?" she asked.

"Of course."

Sailor's lips turned up. "Nellie did it in seventy-two days. For real."

Cruz was impressed.

They made their way through the stacks, passing life-size bronze statues of groundbreaking explorers such as Galileo, Sir Francis Drake, and Lewis and Clark. They took a slight right at Nellie as Mr. Rook had instructed. Near the natural science section, they saw the six-foot crystal pyramid inscribed with the names of the North Star winners. Cruz wanted to stop and read the plaque at the base, but it was almost seven o'clock.

Inside the classroom, they found 24 chairs—one for each student— arranged in a semicircle of two rows. The front wall of the room was made up of nine thin computer screens. The middle screen read WELCOME TO THE ACADEMY. Everybody found seats. Cruz took the second to last chair in the second row, between Sailor and Emmett. When the red numbers on the digital clock in the corner changed from 6:59 to 7:00, everyone got quiet. Five minutes went by. Then ten. Soon, a low murmur went through the room.

"Did they forget we were here?" Zane wondered aloud what they were all thinking.

"Maybe our teacher had car trouble," said Emmett.

"Or is sick," offered Renshaw, on the other side of Sailor.

The knot in Cruz's stomach tightened. Something wasn't right. They were elite explorers, invited from the four corners of the globe to the most prestigious school in the world. The Academy wouldn't forget them—not on their first day. Would they?

At 16 minutes after seven, Dugan Marsh stood up from his seat in the middle of the first row. "I'm going to go tell Mr. Rook."

"Good idea," said a girl in front of Cruz with wavy shoulder-length hair the color of marshmallows.

"Be right back," said Dugan, sprinting for the door.

"Wait!" called Cruz, a thought popping into his head.

Dugan spun. Seeing Cruz, he scowled. "What? Gonna call your aunt for help?"

Cruz felt his face catch fire. "I meant, what if they want us to wait?"

"For what?" snapped Dugan.

Cruz didn't know for sure, but he felt they ought to take a minute to think things through. That's what he did with Aunt Marisol's coded puzzles. Sometimes something that made no sense at first could click into place after you considered it for a bit.

"It could be the opposite," said Zane. "Maybe they want us to *do* something."

"You mean this is some kind of test?" asked Ali.

Cruz nodded. That's what he was beginning to think it was.

"It *is* Explorer Academy," said Emmett.

"We should look around for clues," said Cruz. "Maybe there's something here that will tell us where our teacher is or what we're supposed to do next."

"That's the dumbest thing I've ever heard," said Dugan. "You guys can do whatever you want, but I'm going to get the librarian." He stalked out of the room.

For a few minutes, everyone stayed put. Finally, Cruz stood up. It wouldn't hurt, he figured, to hunt for a clue or two. He turned his chair over but didn't find anything out of the ordinary. Emmett followed his lead. Then Sailor. Soon, the whole class was on their feet, flipping their chairs. From there, everyone fanned out and began scouring the room for hints. Cruz checked the back table and the windowsill. Still nothing. Turning from the window, he straightened. That's when he saw it. How could he have been so blind? Cruz snickered to himself.

"Something funny?" It was the tall girl with arctic white hair. She was pretty and wore a white long-sleeved tee, which made her pale skin look even paler.

"I was thinking: What if our clue has been right in front of us all along?"

Pastel blue eyes widened. "Where?"

Cruz pointed to the wall of screens.

"'Welcome to the Academy.'" As she read the words out loud, Cruz detected a Nordic accent. "Yeah? So?"

"Someone said it to me when I got here last night," he said. "I was thinking maybe she said it to everyone else, too."

"'Welcome to the Academy'?" She gasped. "*Já!* It's Taryn!"

"I ... I could be wrong."

"Hey, everybody, this guy figured it out," shouted the girl, grabbing Cruz by the hand. "We've got to go to Taryn."

Too late for second thoughts now.

Jogging through the library, the girl turned to him. "You're Cruz, aren't you?" When he nodded, she smiled, a dimple appearing on each side of her mouth. "My name is Bryndis Jónsdóttir. I'm from Reykjavík. You?"

"Hawaii."

"Talk about two different worlds. It's probably totally unoriginal to ask this, but do you surf?"

"I love to. We run a surf shop on Kauai."

"Too weird! My parents own a surfing tour business."

"In Iceland?"

She crossed a blue eye in. "Yeah, I know."

"Isn't the water in the North Atlantic kind of cold?"

"Not as cold as everyone always thinks. Right now, water temps are about the same as in Scotland. It's the best time of the year to surf."

Surfing in Iceland sounded fun! Cold, but fun ...

As the class scurried down the wide marble corridor, Cruz hoped his hunch about the clue was correct. If he was off base, he'd have some pretty mad classmates on his hands, including Dugan. He glanced behind him. Maybe he should let someone else take over. Marching toward the lobby with Emmett on one side and Bryndis on the other, there was no way Cruz could pull up and let everyone slip past. With the momentum of the eager crowd pushing him forward, he was stuck in the lead, right or wrong. Crossing his fingers, Cruz hoped for right.

At the sight of the group of new students lining up at her front desk, Taryn clicked her tongue. "Finally! Thirty-seven minutes. Not the best time, explorers."

Twenty-three heads dropped.

"Not the worst, either," she added. "Ready for your next clue?"

Twenty-three heads popped back up. It was all Cruz could do to keep from letting out a cheer. He had been right!

"Listen carefully," said Taryn. "I will say it only once."

Hubbard, who had been napping in a round red-and-gray-plaid bed at the corner of the desk, cocked an ear.

Flipping open the cover on his tablet, Cruz tapped the button to start recording. Emmett gave an approving nod.

Taryn cleared her throat. "Come visit me in Mexico where giant crystals grace. Trek to frigid Iceland where I roam from place to place. Look for me in France where old art is on display. Seek me in New Zealand; let the insects light your way."

Cruz stood dumbfounded. This puzzle wasn't going to be easy.

"Hey!" cried some of the kids when Taryn turned away. "We didn't catch all of that. Can you repeat it?"

"Sorry. Can't. Good luck!"

His eyeglasses aqua circles, Emmett motioned for Cruz, Sailor, and Bryndis to gather around. "Taryn mentioned Iceland and New Zealand. Who's a famous person in those countries that fits the descriptions she gave?"

"Someone who roams from place to place?" Bryndis bit her lip. "There are legends about trolls and elves in Iceland, but I don't think it's the same in France or New Zealand..." She trailed off.

Sailor was shaking her head.

Cruz had visited his great uncle in Mexico City a few years ago, but hadn't seen anything to do with crystals. Looking around, it was obvious the rest of the class was struggling to solve the riddle, too. "Maybe if we heard it again," Cruz said to his friends, who agreed.

Huddling even closer, they listened to his recording of Taryn.

Sailor clamped her hand around Cruz's arm. "Insects that light up. She couldn't be talking about . . . Could she? No, I'm probably on the wrong track—"

"Say it," prompted Cruz. "Even if it sounds silly."

"Once, my family went hiking at this place on the North Island called Waitomo," said Sailor. "We took a boat tour down the river into these caves, and inside the place was lit up by thousands of glowworms."

Emmett and Cruz caught each other's eye. They knew the answer to the riddle!

"The Cave of the Crystals is in Mexico," said Emmett. "And the Lascaux Cave in France has hundreds of Stone Age cave paintings of animals."

Bryndis had caught on, too. "The Skaftafell ice caves in Iceland are part of a glacier, so they are always moving."

"It's the CAVE," Sailor said with a gasp. "That's where we're supposed to go."

They spread the word among their classmates. Everybody bolted for the stairs at the opposite end of the lobby.

"What about Dugan?" asked Zane.

"What about him?" Renshaw shot over his shoulder. "*He* left *us*, remember? This ought to take some of the wind out of his sails."

Maybe, thought Cruz, but it didn't feel right to leave Dugan behind. Besides, hadn't Renshaw been the one to tell him that everyone here helped everyone else? Cruz pulled up. "You guys go on ahead. Dugan probably went back to the library classroom. I'll get him. We'll catch up."

Emmett shook his head. "Cruz, if you're late—"

"We won't be. We'll only be a few minutes behind you." Cruz was already rushing across the lobby. As he skidded around the corner into the hallway, he saw an arm shoot out. Fingers locked on to the front of his shirt and spun him around so fast he nearly went airborne. Cruz's spine hit cold stone. He heard the air whoosh from his lungs.

"You should slow down," said a scratchy male voice. "Somebody could get hurt."

The air knocked out of him, Cruz could only let out a mouse squeak.

"Don't worry, Cruz. I'm not going to hurt you. I'm trying to warn you."

A million questions bombarded his brain. Who was this guy? How did he know him? Warn him? About what?

The man relaxed his grip. Cruz saw that his wrist was blotchy and red, the skin resembling a wrinkled sheet. Glancing up into the shadows, Cruz saw more dark red, crinkly scars on the man's neck. "You need to leave the Academy," hissed the man.

"Leave?" Cruz croaked. "I just got here. I'm one of the new explorers—"

"Yeah, I know. I'm sorry about that, but it can't be helped. You can't stay. It's only a matter of time before they get to you."

The image of a scuba diver flashing in his brain, Cruz shivered.

"Do yourself a favor and get on the next flight back to Hawaii," said the man. "Don't make the same mistake your mother did."

"My . . . mother? How do you know my mother?"

"We used to work together. Petra would be alive today if she had listened to me. I'll tell you what I told her: You cannot win. They are too powerful."

"Who?"

"Nebula," he snapped. "Don't you see? No, of course you don't. Nebula can't take the risk that you—"

They heard footsteps.

"Cruz, listen to me. They killed your mother. They will not hesitate to kill you, too."

6

CRUZ stumbled down the corridor toward the library, the words still echoing in his head.

They killed your mother. They will not hesitate to kill you, too.

His mind was reeling. Could it be true that his mother's death wasn't an accident? Who was Nebula? Did they really kill his mom? And where did Cruz fit into the picture? He was a little kid when his mother had died. What had the scarred man started to say? *Nebula can't take the risk that you—*

Risk? What could a 12-year-old possibly do that would be a threat to anybody? It made no sense. Cruz tried to calm himself as he made his way through the stacks in the library. Should he tell someone? Probably. But who? His aunt was the one person he knew he could trust, but if he told her, she'd tell his dad. The two of them would ship him home in a heartbeat. Threat or no threat, Cruz had no intention of leaving the Academy.

Lani. She would help him sort through things. Right now, however, Cruz needed to find Dugan and get to the CAVE. Cruz spotted his classmate standing in the empty classroom. Dugan's hands were stuffed in his pockets and he was scuffing his toe on the carpet in frustration. He looked to Cruz like the kid on the playground who nobody would invite to play.

"Dugan, come on!" Cruz tried not to shout.

The moment Dugan saw Cruz, the sneer returned.

"We're supposed to go to the CAVE," called Cruz. "Everyone else is already there."

"The CAVE? Well, duh, I *knew* that. I was ... uh ... doubling back to make sure they weren't trying to trick us." Dugan puffed up like one of those inflatable holiday decorations, but Cruz knew the truth: Dugan Marsh wasn't nearly as self-assured as he pretended to be.

"Sure." Cruz rolled his eyes unseen. Even if Dugan didn't appreciate it, Cruz was glad he'd come back for him.

Nearing the nook in the hallway where he'd been grabbed, Cruz took a quick look out of the corner of his eye. The nook was empty. There was no sign of the scarred man.

Cruz and Dugan rushed down the steps and into the basement. Down a corridor they came upon two black doors with a sign above them: COMPUTER ANIMATED VIRTUAL EXPERIENCE. Cruz waved his gold Open Sesame band in front of the security camera. Several weighty bolts unlatched and the doors parted.

The pair stepped into an empty room that was at least the size of a football field—maybe larger. It was difficult to gauge the dimensions because the walls, floor, and even the ceiling were black. Their classmates were sitting on stools roughly 10 yards ahead. An older woman with white, spiked hair stood before them. Lit from above by a single spotlight, she wore a hunter green blazer with a brown velvet collar, chestnut brown jodhpurs, and brown leather riding boots. This had to be Dr. Hightower, the Academy president. She caught sight of Cruz and Dugan and motioned for them to join the group. "It appears we have some latecomers." Her tone indicated she was not pleased with their tardiness. Cruz scrambled onto the stool Emmett had saved for him. Dugan took the spot next to Cruz. Turning on his tablet to take notes, Cruz kept his head low. Slowly lifting his eyes, he saw a line of adults standing in the shadows behind Dr. Hightower. Aunt Marisol was on the far end in a sapphire blue blazer, a long white scarf looped several times around her neck. She had her arms folded tightly across her chest and was frowning in his direction.

Uh-oh.

"You are not here because you are smarter or stronger or braver than others," said Dr. Hightower. "You are not here because you have more perseverance, ambition, or potential." Her gaze locked on to Cruz. "You are not here to prove yourself."

A tremor went through him.

"You are here because the world needs you as much as you need it." The Academy president began to slowly pace. The spotlight traveled with her. "As you go through your training, it may seem like your instructors are asking a great deal from you, perhaps more than you expected to give. We are. We *must.* The future of this planet is in your hands, and you must do better with it than those who have gone before. It is our job to guide you, to help you seek truth and realize your potential. Each class is assigned a set of instructors."

She held out an arm toward the adults standing behind her. "This is yours. They will remain with you throughout your entire education at the Academy. You are privileged to have one of the best faculty ever assembled. You will not meet a more accomplished or dedicated group of experts in his or her respective fields. Allow me to introduce them. This is Dr. Kalpak Modi, geography and astronomy; Dr. Conrad Ishikawa, biology and oceanography." As each professor stepped forward, he or she was illuminated by a separate spotlight. "Dr. Brent Gabriel, conservation and scientific innovations; Dr. Kira Benedict, art and journalism; Dr. Romain Legrand, fitness and survival training; and Dr. Marisol Coronado, anthropology, paleontology, and cryptology. Explorers, this is your faculty. And, faculty, these are your explorers."

Teachers and students applauded one another. When Cruz caught Aunt Marisol's eye, the corners of her mouth turned up. *Whew!* He was forgiven.

When everyone quieted down, Dr. Hightower looked up into the infinite darkness. "So why did we bring you to the CAVE this morning?"

Were they supposed to venture a guess? Cruz had no idea what they were doing here. He didn't want to put his hand up and be wrong, so he kept his head low.

Snork.

At the sound of what sounded sort of like a cow mooing, Cruz's head spun toward the obvious culprit: Dugan. He was about to shush him when he heard another short moo, and this one, he knew, did not come from his classmate. Cruz glanced right. *Emmett?* He heard an odd rumbling noise, like distant thunder. Looking ahead, Cruz's jaw dropped. Were those animals ... and were they ...?

They were! A herd of wildebeests was galloping straight for them! Cruz's chair began to shake. His teeth rattled. The noise was deafening. Dust clouding his vision, Cruz started to dive for cover.

Emmett caught his arm. "It's not real," he called above the roar of hooves.

Cruz coughed. "But the dirt—"

"It's piped in." He pointed to the floor. "Look!"

Wiping his eyes, Cruz saw that Emmett was right. Brown smoke was being blown in from vents underneath them. Once he stood his ground, Cruz realized the roar was coming from speakers above and that the stampede was a three-dimensional video being projected in front of them. When the scene faded and the dust settled, only Cruz, Emmett, Zane, and Sailor were still perched on their chairs. The rest of the explorers were clinging to one another, cowering under their stools, or glued to the exit doors. Next to Cruz, Dugan was flat on his stomach, clutching the legs of his chair for dear life.

"The CAVE—it's the next best thing to being there." Emmett sounded like a commercial.

"No kidding," said Cruz, his heart still threatening to burst through his chest.

As everyone scrambled back to their seats, Cruz noticed Dr. Hightower trying to hide a grin. He wondered how many classes before theirs had fallen for this same ploy.

"So, Jovan told you orientation was easy, did he?" Cruz teased Renshaw when he shuffled past. Renshaw was one of those who had made a dash for the exit.

Renshaw rubbed his sleeve across his mouth. "Brothers."

"You are sitting inside a technological masterpiece, a true wonder of science." Dr. Hightower's voice echoed through the massive chamber. "You may have heard about the Computer Animated Virtual Experience. After all, it's almost impossible to keep something like this a secret. However, while many people may know of this simulator's existence, very few know its mysteries. And we intend to keep it that way. The information I am about to share regarding how the CAVE operates is not to be revealed to anyone beyond these walls—not your friends back home, not even your family."

Cruz and Emmett exchanged eager grins.

"The CAVE is a feast for the senses," continued the Academy president. "It combines holographic imagery, thermal radiation sensory technology, three-dimensional printing, and climate controls."

A holographic cherry tree in bloom appeared beside her. "Much of what you see in here will be programmed computerized images, but touch some of those images"—she reached for a pink blossom—"and the heat from your body will react with the image to produce a sensation. In other words, you can feel something that does not exist!"

The explorers gasped.

"Other objects you'll encounter *will* be solid," she went on to explain. Cruz saw a red flicker. A cardinal landed on Dr. Hightower's shoulder. She held out her finger and the red bird climbed on. "This little robotic creature was created with a 3-D printer and is outfitted with a computer chip and a solar battery."

"No!" hissed Cruz.

"Yes!" gasped Emmett.

Dr. Hightower lifted her hand and the bird flew toward the rafters. "Small solids like this bird can be constructed in a matter of minutes to coincide with your mission or match the choices you make. Put your hand into an outcrop and you may get bitten by a 3-D snake. Of course, as you now know, none of the animals in this environment will harm you, but other things can pose a danger." She gestured to the floor vents. "Atmospheric conditions inside the CAVE are real. In here, you can experience everything from heat exhaustion to frostbite. You can also get injured, so it's important you follow all instructions. This is *not* a game. We do this because it's important for you to learn to handle such situations in here so you can confidently do it out there, where it's life and death. Is that clear?"

Everyone nodded.

"Soon you will board *Orion,* the flagship of the Academy's fleet," said Dr. Hightower. "As you circumnavigate the globe and weigh anchor at various ports, you will assist with research, exploration, conservation, sustainability efforts, and other projects. Preparation is key. You must learn proper techniques, safety procedures, and respect for the areas you'll be visiting. So, for the next month, your education will include classroom work upstairs and training missions down here." She reached to take a clipboard from Professor Modi. "We will be dividing you into four teams of six for your training: Team Magellan, Team Cousteau, Team Galileo, and Team Earhart. Once you have your teams, your teachers will rotate assigning you training missions to complement your coursework. Here we go! Team Magellan will be made up of these six explorers: Ali Soliman, Ekaterina Pajarin, Zane Patrick, Matteo Montefiore, Yulia Navarro, and Tao Sun..."

Cruz wanted to be on the same team as Emmett, but with a one-in-four chance, the odds were against him.

"Team Cousteau will be comprised of the following students," said the Academy president. "Emmett Lu, Renshaw McKittrick..."

Cruz held his breath.

"Sailor York, Bryndis Jónsdóttir..."

Shoot! He wasn't going to make it.

"...Cruz Coronado..."

Yes! Cruz put his fist out to the side. Emmett bumped it with his own.

"Getting on the same team as your roommate," spit Dugan out of the side of his mouth. "Gee, I wonder how that happened?"

"...and Dugan Marsh," said Dr. Hightower.

In an instant, Emmett's round glasses went from buttercup yellow to battleship gray, causing Cruz to stifle a chuckle. Maybe wearing your emotions on your face wasn't such a brilliant idea after all. Cruz understood how Emmett felt. Dugan had made it perfectly clear he didn't think Cruz belonged here. As a teammate, Dugan wasn't likely to cut him any slack. Cruz would have to stay on his toes.

The moment Dr. Hightower finished announcing the teams, all the lights in the CAVE went out. A hush fell over the room. They were in complete darkness, unable to see even an inch in front of their eyes. Cruz clutched his stool so he wouldn't fall. Was it a power outage?

"Explorers, you are here because you have earned the privilege." Dr. Hightower's voice floated to them. "You are top scholars, creative thinkers, and talented individuals. On paper, there can be no debate, you are extraordinary. But..." She left the word hanging.

A message began to appear several feet above the stage, the glowing white words hovering in the air like a banner in the breeze:

WITH ALL, COOPERATION. FOR ALL, RESPECT. ABOVE ALL, HONOR.

"...what of your character?" asked Dr. Hightower softly. "The motto you see above me is the cornerstone on which the Academy was founded in 1888. It is the very foundation of who we are and what we stand for. In fact, you will find these words inscribed in stone not far from where you sit. As you embark together on your journey, as you seek the truth and serve the world, I expect you to hold yourselves to the highest standards of integrity, honesty, and compassion. And I am confident you will."

They watched the message slowly vanish, like salt dissolving in water. By the time the words were gone, Cruz had committed them to memory.

Dr. Hightower then announced there would be a 10-minute break, after which everyone was to meet back in the library classroom for their first class at 8 a.m., Intro to Conservation with Professor Gabriel.

"One final thought," she said as the lights came up. "*Fortes fortuna adiuvat.* It's a Latin phrase. Who can tell me what it means?"

Emmett raised his hand, and when called on answered, "Fortune favors the brave."

"Correct." Dr. Hightower opened her arms. "Now go, truth seekers. Discover. Innovate. Protect. The world awaits you."

Leaping to their feet, the new explorers applauded. No one clapped louder or longer than Cruz. Dr. Hightower was right. Cruz was in charge of his own destiny. No one else. He would seek truth. He would serve the world. He would make a difference.

All he had to do now was stay alive.

7

"I'M IN one piece—see?" Cruz wiggled the fingers on both hands. "It's been four days since he warned me and nothing bad has happened."

Lani leaned forward, turning the screen of Cruz's tablet into one large brown eyeball. "I still don't like it. I've been worried ever since you told me. I think you should do what the guy said and come home."

"That's silly. I don't even know who he is, except that he claims to have worked with my mother."

"Cruz. When a big scary man with scars tells you someone is out to get you, I don't care who he is. You should listen."

Cruz picked his tablet up off his desk and crossed to his bed. How could he make her understand? He'd wanted to believe he could attend the Academy like any average explorer, but it was impossible. He *wasn't* your average explorer. His mother had worked for the Society. She had died for it. No, she'd been *killed* for it. If it took the rest of his life, Cruz knew he had to dig and dig until he uncovered the truth. And right now? He needed his best friend's help. "Please, Lani?"

She let out an irritated sigh. "Fine. What do you want me to do?"

"The man said Nebula was behind my mom's death. I have no idea who or what Nebula is, although he did use the word 'they.' He said 'they' would be after me. The problem is, everyone here is monitored." Cruz held up his wrist to show her his OS band. "If I start poking around, even on my tablet, somebody's bound to notice."

"All right, I'll check it out. Do you think your mom was working on a project for this … Nebula?"

"If she had been, it would have been top secret."

"Would your mom have told your aunt anything about it?"

"I doubt it, but I can ask. We've got our first CAVE training mission this afternoon. I'll talk to Aunt Marisol after that." Cruz clicked his tongue against the roof of his mouth. "I have to be careful what I say, though. If my aunt thought my life was in danger—"

"She'd send you home faster than you can say *Orion*," finished Lani.

"You're not going to tell my dad about the warning, are you?"

"I should."

"But you won't."

She twisted the ends of her hair. "But I won't."

"Thanks, Lani."

"Don't make me regret it. If you get yourself killed, I'm going to be so mad at you."

"I won't."

"So now that it's Friday, how was your first week?"

"Intense! I've already got heaps of homework in every class, even fitness and survival training! Monsieur Legrand used to be in the military. Plus, along with our regular classes and CAVE training, we're required to take a 'fun' class twice a week." He made air quotes when he said the word "fun." "You know, like a foreign language or cooking."

Lani choked. "Cooking? You?"

"I signed up for flight school."

"Smart. You don't want to burn the place down your first week there. Makes kind of a bad impression."

Cruz pretended to smack the screen.

"Hi, guys!" Sailor appeared in the doorway. "Ready to go virtual exploring?"

Cruz motioned for Sailor to come in. "Emmett will be right back. He was going to get Taryn to run him to the store for socks."

"Socks? Already?"

"The guy goes through three pairs a day—something about having hot feet—and we don't do laundry until tomorrow," explained Cruz.

"Why didn't he cadge from you?"

Cruz twisted his mouth as he tried to figure out her slang.

"Borrow," translated Sailor, sensing his confusion. "Why didn't Emmett borrow some from you?"

"I offered, but he said there are three things a person should never borrow: socks, underwear, or a toothbrush."

Sailor giggled. "He'd better hurry. On my way here, I passed Renshaw and Dugan heading to the CAVE. Bryndis has already gone down. She wanted to play with Hubbard first."

"Uh, Cruz?" Lani was trying to look around Cruz.

"Sorry, Lani, this is Sailor York. She's one of my Cousteau teammates." Cruz lifted his tablet. "Sailor, this is Lani Kealoha, my best friend from back home."

The girls waved to each other.

"Lani made me this micro remote for my honeybee drone." Cruz tugged on the front of his shirt to show Sailor the honeycomb pin. "Mell, turn on." The bee sitting on his desk blinked, its eyes changing from dull black to gold lights.

"Sweet as!"

"Sailor's from New Zealand. It's a Kiwi thing," said Cruz before Lani could ask.

"You must be super smart," Sailor said into the tablet's camera.

"Nah," said Lani.

"She is," said Cruz.

"Sorry, sorry, sorry," said Emmett, flying into the room.

"Hiya, Emmett," called Lani.

"Hi, Lani." He was ripping open a package of socks with his teeth. As he pulled them out of the bag, two sloth faces stared at Cruz and Sailor. The pair shot each other looks.

"It was all they had!" Emmett kicked off his shoes. "Taryn didn't have time to take me to the store. I had to go to the museum gift shop."

The mail icon was flashing on Cruz's tablet. It was a message from Dr. Gabriel:

> *Technical issue at the main entrance to the CAVE. Meet at the north entrance instead. From your floor, take the back stairs to the basement, go left, then take the second right. Look for the silver door.*

"I'd better go," Cruz said to Lani.

"Be careful," she said, and he promised he would.

They said their goodbyes. Cruz turned off Mell and set it on the windowsill.

As Cruz and Sailor waited for Emmett, they read over their instructions again. The email from Dr. Gabriel told them to plan for the weather in the CAVE to be around 60 degrees and windy. They were directed to bring water bottles and their tablets, and not to enter the simulator until all team members were present.

"Let's jet," said Emmett, bouncing to his feet.

Cruz grabbed his coat, water, and tablet, and they were off. Rushing down the back stairs, Cruz's pulse quickened. This was it! In a few minutes, he would be in the CAVE on his first Explorer Academy training mission. Once in the basement, the trio followed Dr. Gabriel's directions and easily found the silver door. A piece of paper was taped to it. *CAVE* was scrawled on the page in red ink.

Cruz waved his OS band in front of the security camera. The door didn't move.

"Yours must not be working," said Sailor, trying hers. Again, nothing. "Maybe they forgot to give us security clearance at this entrance?"

"Maybe," said Cruz, but it didn't seem likely.

"Something's wrong." Emmett stepped up to the door. "Our bands won't work here. This isn't a standard security cam." Taking off his glasses, he got up on tiptoe to get close to the lens. "This is an IBI system."

"Iris biometric identification?" Cruz watched a thin red beam shoot out of the camera and scan Emmett's eyeball. Cruz knew the iris of the eye is like a fingerprint—no two are alike.

The red beam shut off. The door did not open.

Putting on his glasses, Emmett flipped open the cover of his tablet. "I'll pull up the campus map. Maybe we're at the wrong spot."

"We're going to be late," moaned Sailor.

"It'll only take a minute."

They heard footsteps in the hallway behind them.

"Cracker!" cried Sailor. "Finally, someone who can give us directions. Be right back." She hurried toward the sound.

Cruz was tapping at his own tablet to retrieve the message from Dr. Gabriel. Maybe he'd gotten the directions wrong. "I can't seem to log on."

"Me neither." Emmett spun his screen. "The server must be down, or maybe there's no Wi-Fi down here—"

"Hey!" A cry echoed through the hall.

Cruz glanced at Emmett. "What was that?"

"I don't know..."

Suddenly, Sailor was barreling at them. "Bad guy ... Run ..."

"Huh?"

She flew past him so fast he felt a brisk breeze. *"Run!"*

They heard the sharp smack of hard soles against marble and saw a figure charging their way. Exchanging shocked looks, Cruz and Emmett took off after Sailor. They stayed on her tail through the maze of corridors, zipping right, then left, then right again.

"Faster, Emmett!" Cruz shouted as his roommate started to flag. "The footsteps were gaining on them. They sounded like boots. Could they be cowboy boots? Cruz saw Sailor up ahead. She was hanging out an open door. "In here." She waved them inside and whipped the door shut behind them. The trio gasped for air.

It smelled like ammonia. Next to him, Emmett's glasses began to emit a soft purple light, revealing that they had taken refuge in a janitorial supply closet. Cruz stared at the glowing frames. "How do you—"

"Shhh-shhh-shhh!" Sailor had her ear to the door.

The steps slowed … They were stopping right outside … This was it … They were going to get caught! Cruz fixed his gaze on the doorknob, his heart beating wildly as he watched and waited to see if it would turn.

The footsteps were walking away!

"What happened back there?" Emmett hissed to Sailor.

"I don't know. I started to ask this guy with a badge for directions and he grabbed me. He started dragging me back down the hall. I kicked him in the shins as hard as I could and ran as fast as I bloody could."

"Was he wearing cowboy boots?" asked Cruz.

"I … I don't know. It all happened so fast."

Could this be the same man who had attacked Cruz in Hanalei? Or the one who followed him in the airport? Maybe Lani was right. Maybe Cruz should have listened to the scarred man's warning.

After several tense minutes of silence from the hall, which felt like hours to Cruz, Sailor said, "I'll check to see if the coast is clear." She turned the doorknob. "Crikey! It won't open." She jiggled it again. "We're locked in."

"It's probably jammed," said Cruz. "Let me try."

Sailor stepped aside. Cruz twisted the knob while shoving his shoulder against the door. It didn't budge. With a running start, Cruz threw himself against the door again. He bounced off. Pain shot through his shoulder. "Ow!"

"We're going to miss our training mission," said Sailor. "This is turning into a disaster."

"Don't panic," said Emmett. "I'm sure Professor Gabriel will let us reschedule."

"I'm not," moaned Cruz. "Part of the training is following directions. If we don't get to the CAVE on time, we could fail the whole exercise."

"Fail?" croaked Sailor.

"We'd better call for help." Cruz pulled out his cell phone. He tried texting and calling Taryn, but his attempts were rejected. He turned to his roommate.

Emmett was shaking his head. "No luck. We must be too far down to get a signal."

"This cannot be happening," wailed Sailor. "I've never failed anything in my life."

"Uh...guys?" Emmett was near the door. "I think we've got bigger problems to worry about than our grade."

Cruz couldn't imagine what could possibly be worse than being locked in a storage closet and missing their first training mission. "What?"

"I smell something," said Sailor, sniffing the air. "Pickles. Do you guys smell pickles?"

"Down here," cried Emmett, lowering his computer screen to illuminate the floor.

Tendrils of smoke were curling up from under the door.

"Fire!" cried Sailor. "The building's on fire!"

"No," said Emmett, making a sour face. "It's gas. By the yellow color and the pickle smell, I'd say either kenzotrone or ferbenzogene. Get away from the door."

They stepped back. As the yellow fog enveloped them, they began to cough. Cruz's eyes and throat were starting to burn.

"Coats...Give me your coats," gasped Sailor.

Turning, Cruz held his arms out so she could pull the jacket off his back. Through the haze, he could see her stuffing their clothing between the bottom of the door and the floor.

"Stay low," cried Emmett, his voice muffled by the sleeve he held against his mouth.

Cruz sank to the floor. Pulling the top of his T-shirt over his chin, his fingers swept over a small, smooth bump.

Mell!

It was a long shot, to be sure. *If* the drone's remote control radio frequency wasn't being jammed and *if* it was in range and *if* it could manage to slip under all the doors between his dorm room and here and *if* the toxic gas didn't affect its machinery, Mell *might* be able to use its stinger to unlock the door. There was also the possibility that the whole floor was flooded with gas and even *if* they got out, they wouldn't make it any farther than a few feet into the corridor. But it was their only hope. He had to give it a try.

"Mell, turn on," he wheezed. "Mell, lock on to my coordinates . . . Come to me . . . Unlock the door . . ."

Sailor and Emmett were huddled in the other corner. His vision blurring, Cruz couldn't tell if his friends were still conscious. Mell might be able to unlock the door, but it certainly couldn't open it. Somebody—Cruz—had to get to the door.

Cruz pulled his shirt up over his nose. He flipped onto his belly. The moment his chest hit the floor, something within him relaxed. His body didn't need to be told what to do. After all the years of surfing, it knew. Cruz pushed himself along the marble floor of the storage room and thought of the warm turquoise surf of Hanalei Bay. If this was what death was like—remembering good times in better places—it could be worse. Moments later, Cruz heard a noise on the other side of the door. It sounded like Mell's buzz. His MAV had made it!

Cruz reached up into the fog for the doorknob. His chest on the verge of exploding, he needed both hands to pull himself up to his knees.

He heard the latch click. Mell had done it! All Cruz had to do to free them was turn the knob . . . but did it go right or left? His thoughts had become jumbled puzzle pieces in a box and he couldn't seem to pick one out.

Right . . . Yes, right! Turn it right . . . a little more . . .

The door opened and Cruz fell through it onto the cold marble floor, gulping in as much fresh air as his lungs could handle. *Fresh air!* The hall was clear. After a few breaths to get oxygen to his muddled brain, Cruz turned back for Emmett and Sailor. They were coming through the cloud on their hands and knees. Reaching an arm out to each one, Cruz dragged them into the hall. It took everyone a few minutes to stop gagging.

"That was . . . close," coughed Emmett. His glasses were the tiniest of black slits. Sweat glued his shirt to his chest.

"I don't . . . get it," gasped Sailor. "If it's okay out here . . . then how did the gas get—" She stopped, her eyes following Cruz's gaze.

They watched a white tank about the size of a liter of soda slowly roll down the corridor.

A pain stabbing his temple, Cruz squinted at Sailor. "Was the ... door to the storage closet open when you found it?"

"Uh ... yeah ... I think so." She frowned. "Are you saying this was deliberate? That someone wanted us to go in there ... so they could do this?"

Cruz started to say that's exactly what he thought, but everything went dark.

8

"IS HE going to be all right?"

"Should be. His vital signs are stable."

Cruz heard voices. They sounded far away.

"Maybe we should call his aunt. Professor Coronado is a teacher here."

"Dr. Marisol Coronado? *She* is *his* aunt? So then he's—"

"Cruz," croaked Cruz. He struggled to open his eyelids. "Coronado."

"Are you okay?" Sailor was kneeling beside him.

"I . . . I think so." His throat felt like it had been through a shredder. Blinking, Cruz saw he was in a white office stretched out on a white sofa with a cushion under his head. Emmett was perched on the opposite arm of the sofa, his brow furrowed. The small office was encased in glass on three sides; however, tinted windows kept them from seeing out. The door was closed. When he saw the red dot of a security camera mounted in the ceiling blinking at him, Cruz bolted up. "Mell!"

"It's okay," said Sailor, patting her pocket. "I've got her."

"Her?"

"Mell has a stinger, right?" She gave him a smirk. "Only female honeybees have stingers."

Sailor *was* correct. Cruz didn't care if Mell was a girl or boy as long as it was safe.

"You look more like yourself again," Emmett said to him. "I've never seen anyone turn the color of a prehnite crystal before."

Cruz gave him a small grin. Prehnite crystals were green.

"Fortunately, Dr. Miles came along and—"

"Jericho," said the man. He had his back to them, and Cruz could see a long blond ponytail hanging down the back of a white lab coat. "Call me Jericho. I've never been one for titles. Good thing you got out of that supply closet when you did. Another few minutes and ..."

"Jericho brought us here," said Sailor. "Well, he carried you."

"Where are we?" asked Cruz.

"In my office," said Jericho. "It's ... uh ... next to the chemistry lab for upper-level explorers."

A student lab? With tinted windows and two—no, three security cameras? Cruz wasn't buying it.

"Here." Jericho held out a beaker-like glass to Cruz. It contained a murky purple liquid. Holding it up to the light, Cruz saw what appeared to be gel beads bobbing.

"I'm okay, thanks," he said. He wasn't in the habit of accepting a strange potion offered to him by a strange person, especially when that person had told him a lie the size of a great white shark.

"Drink it," said Jericho. "It'll counteract the effects of the ferbenzogene. FBZ can pack quite a punch."

"It's all right," said Emmett, but Cruz hesitated. "We had some, too. It helps."

Sailor nodded.

Cruz wrapped his fingers around the glass. He took a small sip. The lukewarm liquid wasn't bad. It tasted like apples. The gel blobs popping on his tongue released a cinnamon flavor.

"It'll take about ten minutes to kick in," said Jericho. "In the meantime, I'll go check in with my . . . students and be back to take you upstairs."

"Thanks, but we should go now," said Cruz, swinging his legs to the floor. "We've got to get to the CAVE for training—"

"You're in no shape to go anywhere, especially the CAVE."

Cruz didn't argue. He felt like he was on a moving carousel.

"It's too late anyway," said Emmett. "We missed our slot."

"Back in a few," said Jericho. Opening the door, he nodded to Cruz. "Down the hatch."

Cruz put the beaker to his lips. They watched Jericho leave. The fact that he locked them in after shutting the door did not escape anyone's notice.

The moment they were alone, Sailor blurted, "We're in the Synthesis."

Cruz nearly spit out his drink. He knew Jericho had lied to them but *the Synthesis*? No way. Not possible. Cruz's dad had once told him that helping to form the Synthesis was his mother's greatest achievement and her biggest secret. The lab was so confidential only a handful of people outside the Society even knew of its existence. It was not something a person—or in this case, three people—could have stumbled into, and if by some crazy chance they had, Jericho Miles certainly would not have brought them *inside.* How would Sailor know about the Synthesis anyway?

"This is the most classified lab in the world," hissed Emmett. "This is where they're stretching the boundaries of human capabilities. I'm talking cybernetics and superpowers—real cutting-edge stuff. Do you realize only the president of the United States and a few Cabinet members even know about this place and we are *IN IT*?"

"Yeah?" said Cruz, trying to keep his voice light. "If it's so classified, how do *you* know about it?"

Emmett lifted his chin as if offended at the question. "I just do."

"I thought you said we needed top secret clearance to get in . . ."

"I guess almost dying from a lethal dose of poison gas right outside the door works, too," said Sailor drily.

"But Jericho said—"

"He's lying," snapped Emmett, hopping to his feet. "On the way in we saw more than enough evidence to prove this *is* the Synthesis: IBIs and twelve-code deadlatch cipher locks, Apocalypse Four Thousand-XD bio suits, steel-reinforced pneumatic doors. And then there's that stuff you're drinking."

Cruz glanced at the beaker in his hands.

"No high school chem lab, not even the Academy's, has the antidote for ferbenzogene," said Emmett. "Most *hospitals* don't even carry it. You have to keep it in a special refrigeration unit at twenty-two degrees Fahrenheit with direct exposure to sunlight, or the plankton microbeads will break down and be completely useless—"

"All right." Cruz raised a hand in surrender. The carousel may have slowed, but he was still too woozy to process Emmett's intricate explanations.

"Of course, we still don't know why that guy was after us," said Emmett, inspecting Jericho's computer. He tapped at a few keys, but it wasn't asleep. It had been turned off.

"It's me they're after," said Cruz. "Not you."

"Why?" Emmett and Sailor said in unison.

"I'm not exactly sure." Cruz hadn't planned on involving anyone else in his troubles, but it was a little late for that now, wasn't it? "I'll tell you what I know," he said. And he did. He told them about his mother's lab accident and the encounter with the scarred man in the hallway on orientation day. Cruz did not tell them about his birthday letter. Some things he wanted to keep to himself.

"I'm so sorry about your mom." Sailor's voice was gentle.

"Me too," said Emmett, shaking his head. "Terrible thing to have happen."

"Thanks." Feeling his chest tighten, Cruz quickly drained his glass.

"I knew there was something weird about that guy at the airport," said Emmett. "Do you think he was with . . . this Nebula that was after your mom?"

"Could be," said Cruz.

"So what do we do now?" asked Sailor.

"*You* guys are going to do nothing," said Cruz. "I don't know why Nebula has a target on my back, but I don't want anything to happen to you because of me. I've just got to figure this out on my own. Sorry, Emmett. I probably cost you the North Star award."

Emmett flopped into Jericho's chair. He spun to face the wall. Cruz didn't blame him for being angry.

Biting her lip, Sailor looked at the floor.

Cruz slowly got to his feet. He was shaky but no longer dizzy. Where was Jericho, anyway? Cruz had things to do, like talk to Aunt Marisol about his mom and beg Dr. Gabriel to give Team Cousteau a second chance. Time was ticking away.

"No."

Cruz's ears perked up. "Emmett? Did you say something?"

"I said no." Emmett's voice grew stronger. "I'm not going to let you figure this out—whatever it is—by yourself."

"Me neither," said Sailor. "We need to stick together. We're team-mates, after all."

"And truth seekers," added Emmett, spinning at last to face them.

Cruz and Sailor gasped.

"Emmett, your glasses!" shrieked Sailor.

Emmett's frames were no longer a single color. Now flecks of bright turquoise, peacock, lapis, and a dozen other shades of blue pulsed through teardrop-shaped frames in a rapid-flowing river. Watching the kaleidoscopic heartbeat, Cruz stammered. "I . . . I think they're alive."

His roommate merely gave them a knowing smile.

CRUZ WAS PLAYING A GAME of tug-of-war with Hubbard when he felt a hand latch on to his elbow. He released the short, knotted rope and the energetic Westie took off, racing through the lobby with his prize. "Aunt Marisol, I was on my way to see you—"

"Were you now?" Her tone was sharp.

She knew. She knew they'd missed this afternoon's training session.

"I can explain—"

"Not here." Cotton-candy-pink high heels struck the marble floor with precision as she guided him across the room.

His aunt punched through the door to the courtyard, and suddenly they were bathed in the early evening sunlight. It took Cruz's eyes a moment to adjust. Old oak, maple, and birch trees lined the curved flagstone path, their leaves forming a thick canopy against a vivid blue sky. The trees were starting to change from their summer coats into a fall wardrobe of garnets and golds. Cruz could almost hear Emmett say, *The changing colors are due to a decrease of sunlight and water, along with temperature fluctuations, which cause the trees to stop making chlorophyll, the pigment that gives leaves their green color—*

"Cruz Sebastian Coronado!" Aunt Marisol's eyes were blazing.

Oops. She had said something or asked him a question and he hadn't been paying attention. Not that he needed three guesses to narrow down the topic. "I'm sorry we didn't make it to the CAVE for our mission.

We … uh … got the time wrong. It was my fault." Cruz hated lying to his aunt, but what choice did he have?

"I'm not the one you should be apologizing to."

"I already called Dr. Gabriel." Cruz had called their professor the second Jericho Miles had brought them back upstairs to their hall. "I'm going to see him Monday before class. I'll talk to everyone on the team this weekend, too."

"Good." She started down the path, her heels clacking sharply against the stones. Aunt Marisol's flowing green dress, splattered with pink hibiscus flowers, reminded him of home. Cruz fell into step beside her, waiting for the lecture he knew was to come. "Listen, Cruz, if you don't want to commit to the program—"

"I do."

"If you think you can give less than your best effort and I will bail you out—"

"I don't. Honest, I don't." Cruz bit his tongue. He wanted to tell her what had happened to them in the basement and how close they had come to dying, but knew he couldn't. First, she'd freak out. Once she was done freaking, she'd send him straight home. "I'll do better, Aunt Marisol. I promise."

Her pace slowed, her shoulders dropping from her ears. "I know it seems like I'm being harsh, but you have to understand that people are watching. They're waiting to see if I give you special treatment. Your work must be stellar and your behavior exemplary so there can be no doubt you belong here. It may not seem fair, but—"

"I know. I know they're watching," he said, an image of Dugan flashing in his brain. "You don't need to tell me. I can feel it every day."

"I'm not expecting perfection." Her mouth softened. "If it's any consolation, I wasn't anywhere near the top of my class when I attended the Academy."

"You weren't? I thought Mom and you—"

"Your mother was the standout. I was always playing catch-up. I had to study twice as long and hard as Petra did, but she probably wouldn't want me telling you that. You're under enough pressure and scrutiny as it is."

A thought occurred to him. "She won the North Star award, didn't she?"

"Yes."

"Dad never told me."

"Probably thought it would only encourage you to follow in her footsteps."

"Which he definitely doesn't want me to do."

"Not because he wasn't proud of her," his aunt was quick to say. "But for your own safety. After the accident, things changed. He changed."

Cruz glanced at Aunt Marisol. She had stopped to touch the lacy golden leaves of a Japanese maple. She didn't seem mad anymore. If ever there was a time to ask about his mother's projects with the Synthesis, it was now. Cruz took a minute to gather his courage. "You... uh... always said I could ask you anything about her."

"You can."

"Did she... I mean, do you know what she was working on when she... when the accident happened?"

She turned away from the tree, a vertical line appearing between her eyebrows. "No. Her projects were classified. We never talked about them. Even your dad didn't know. I tried to find out some details after the accident, but I got nowhere. Top secret is top secret forever, I'm afraid."

"Oh. Sure. I get it."

"Is there a reason you're asking? Has someone said something?"

"No," he lied. "I guess it's . . . being here . . . you know, so close to where it happened. I was just . . . wondering."

"I wish I could be of more help." She put an arm around him. "I *can* tell you one thing, Cruz: Your mom was passionate about her work. She was exactly where she wanted to be doing exactly what she wanted to be doing. Everyone should be so lucky."

He knew she was saying it to make him feel better, but it didn't. Who cared if his mom loved her work? Cruz would have rather she did something boring if it meant she'd be alive today. Maybe that was selfish, but that's how he felt.

"You look flushed," she said. "Are you feeling okay?"

"I'm fine," he said. It was true. Cruz rarely got sick. A sniffle here, a slight headache there, though rarely anything worse.

She put a hand to his forehead. "You seem warm. Maybe you should—"

"I'm okay, Aunt Marisol, but thanks," he said, and he meant it. There was something soothing about having your mom or, in this case, your aunt, check your head for fever. It gave him a kind of peace—one he hadn't felt in a long time. Stuffing his hands into his front pockets, Cruz walked backward away from her. "See you tomorrow. Might go take a wee kip."

"Huh?"

"A nap."

"Did you eat dinner?"

"Not yet."

"It's almost six. Eat. And I mean something healthy. Not pie."

"I like pie."

Shaking her head, she slapped a hand over her eyes. The gesture made him smile. His dad did the same thing whenever Cruz exasperated him. Aunt Marisol turned toward the administration building, her swingy dress swirling around her like hibiscus blossoms floating on the water.

Cruz ambled back down the flagstone path toward the Academy. He lifted his head and closed his eyes, letting the sun warm his face. He could almost hear the gentle lapping of the waves back home and feel the toasted sand sift through his toes. It was Friday night. He and Dad always ordered pepperoni and sausage pizza with extra cheese on Fridays. For dessert, they'd have macadamia nut ice cream. Of course, right now it was lunchtime in Hanalei. Cruz wondered if his dad would order a pizza tonight. And have ice cream. Without him.

Tears gathered behind his eyelids. It was silly, really. He had talked to or texted his dad nearly every day since arriving last weekend. Besides, explorers weren't supposed to get homesick. They were supposed to be strong. Daring. Fearless. So how come he always felt the opposite? Tipping his head back, Cruz blinked as fast as humanly possible. He was determined not to let a single tear escape. And none did. Well, maybe a small one.

OYAMEL FOREST
OAXACA, MEXICO

PACIFIC
OCEAN

SIERRA MADRE ORIENTAL

UNITED STATES

MEXICO

GULF OF
MEXICO

YUCATAN
PENINSULA

CUBA

CARIBBEAN
SEA

BELIZE

GUATEMALA

PANAMA

MEETING with Professor Gabriel before class on

Monday morning, Cruz was prepared to do whatever it took to convince
his instructor to give Team Cousteau another shot with their CAVE
mission, even if it meant taking the blame. "It's my fault we missed the
session," he said to his teacher. "Lower my grade or give me extra work
if you want, but please don't punish my team—"

Dr. Gabriel tipped his bald head to peer at him over the top of black
bifocals. "I'm rescheduling the session, Cruz."

That was easy. "Great! Thank you, Dr. Gabriel."

"Don't thank me. Thank Dugan, Renshaw, and Bryndis. They followed
their instructions and did not go into the CAVE without the three of
you. I told them I'd reschedule just for them but they insisted the
whole team stay together. I was impressed by their loyalty, and *that* is
why you are getting a second chance."

"Oh." Cruz picked at his pinkie nail. So much for Cruz Coronado saving the day.

"I do appreciate your apology, though." Dr. Gabriel gave him a half
grin. "I admire an explorer with courage. Let's see if you can continue
that in a leadership role on your team, shall we?"

"Yes. I . . . I mean, I can . . . I *will*."

"That's what I like to hear."

"Let's see . . ." Dr. Gabriel was tipping his head back so he could read his computer screen through his bifocals. "We rescheduled your simulator training for this Thursday at three p.m."

Cruz flipped open the cover on his laptop so he could add it to his calendar. "Can we use the main entrance to the CAVE this time? Is it working now?"

"Well, yes. It's always been working, as far as I know."

"Last Friday it wasn't. That's why you messaged me to use the other entrance, remember?"

"No." His professor looked perplexed. "I did not."

"Yes you did."

"Cruz, I think I would know if I'd messaged you."

"You said there was a technical problem. See?" Cruz showed him the note he'd received moments before his half of Team Cousteau had headed down to the basement.

Dr. Gabriel frowned. "I didn't send that."

Cruz was starting to put the pieces together: the last-minute email, the handwritten sign on the silver door ... It had all been part of a ploy—most likely Nebula's—to lure him into the basement to meet his doom. Thank goodness for Mell and Jericho.

"I'll have the tech crew check into the fake email and find out which prankster will be getting some additional homework this weekend," said Dr. Gabriel. "As for you, Cruz, I don't think I need to tell you: Do not be late for your rescheduled CAVE mission."

"You don't. I won't."

AND CRUZ WASN'T. He was, as a matter of fact, 22 minutes early. Waiting for his teammates to arrive, Cruz reviewed their mission instructions:

DEAR TEAM COUSTEAU MEMBER,
Your first training expedition in the CAVE
is rescheduled for 3–5 p.m. this Thursday.
To prepare, read Dr. Gabriel's assigned text
on conservation. Plan for the weather to be
approximately 60°F and windy. Wear a jacket,
long pants, and sturdy shoes or hiking boots
(no flip-flops!). Bring water and your tablet.
Do not proceed into the simulator without all
team members present. Further instructions
will appear in the CAVE as well as on your
computer (log in to Dr. Gabriel's site).
Be advised, it is against the rules to discuss a
mission or its outcome with any other team.
This is to prevent any team(s) from having an
unfair advantage. Best of luck.
DARE TO EXPLORE!

At seven minutes to three, every member of Team Cousteau had assembled in front of the main entrance to the CAVE.

"We're all here," said Renshaw. He seemed relieved. He held his OS band up to the security camera and the doors parted.

"Must be nice to have an aunt who can pull your butt out of the fire whenever you screw up, huh?" Dugan spat at Cruz.

Cruz felt his blood start to bubble but took a few deep breaths to calm himself. If Dugan was trying to get a rise out of him, Cruz would not give him the satisfaction. Besides, he needed to focus. He had to do well on this mission.

"Here we go," said Sailor, her eyes filled with anticipation.

Cruz knew how she felt. *Finally,* their first training mission. Team Cousteau stepped into the simulator and the doors shut behind them.

Cruz expected to be facing the same mammoth, empty room they'd seen on their first day of class, but this—this was anything but a blank canvas. He was standing in the middle of a forest! Tall firs surrounded him, their lean trunks stretching 50 feet or more into a blue sky. A shaft of sunlight warmed his neck. Lush underbrush tickled his ankles. He caught an earthy whiff of soil and pine in the crisp air. Cruz did a slow circle to take it all in. The landscape was so lifelike ... right down to the gnat buzzing around his ear.

"Incredible!" said Sailor, a breeze ruffling her hair.

"Where are we?" asked Bryndis.

"In the mountains somewhere," said Emmett. "I'd say it's fall, wherever we are. I'll take some weather readings—"

"Look!" said Renshaw.

Ahead of them, a dirt trail had appeared. A yellow arrow hovered like a hummingbird in the middle of the path. It pointed toward the summit.

"The arrow is telling us where to go," said Bryndis.

"I'll take the lead and get us there safely, unless you're going to complain to your aunt, Coronado." Dugan bowed. "Then be my guest."

"Quit being a dingleberry, Dugan," shot Sailor. "We need to work together. We're a team."

Mumbling something about how it wasn't fair that he got stuck on the lamest team ever, Dugan started up the trail.

Hiking up the hill, Cruz tried to figure out how the floor moved and tilted to mimic an actual trail. Were they on a treadmill? Beside him, Emmett was on his computer. "By my calculations, I'd say we're at an elevation between two thousand one hundred and two thousand four hundred meters; that's seven to eight thousand feet, for you. The drop in both oxygen and air pressure is going to tire us out much quicker than if we were at sea level."

"It's definitely harder to breathe." Cruz could tell he was expending more effort here than he did climbing Namolokama Mountain back home, which was 4,400 feet.

"The trail is getting steeper, too," said Emmett. "We should tell

Dugan to slow down so everyone can adjust to—"

"Cruz! Emmett!"

Bryndis and Sailor were 20 yards behind them on the trail. They were standing next to Renshaw. He was bent over, his hands clutching his knees for support.

"Dugan!" Cruz shouted up the trail, but their intrepid leader had already rounded the bend. So much for getting his team there safely.

"I'm ... all right," said Renshaw when Cruz and Emmett reached him. "I just need a second. I have asthma ... the altitude can get to me sometimes. My family ... we're into sports, so I'm used to it. I've got my inhaler with me if it gets worse."

"Did you bring water?" asked Cruz. When Renshaw shook his head, Cruz handed him his own black aluminum bottle.

"Thanks." Renshaw took a few sips. "You guys can go on ahead. I'll catch up with you at the clearing."

"No," said Cruz, brushing away a moth. "We're gonna stay together."

"Okay." Renshaw's lips turned up. "Thanks."

Sailor snickered. "Cruz, you've got a butterfly on your head."

"I do?"

"There's another one," said Bryndis as a pair of orange-and-black wings flitted by. "There's some more in that tree," said Sailor. She spun. "And in that one!"

"They're *everywhere*," said Bryndis.

She was right. The forest was teeming with butterflies.

Cruz knew where they were now! "We're in Mexico, in the—"

"Monarch Butterfly Biosphere Reserve," finished Emmett.

"I've read about this place," said Sailor. "Monarch butterflies migrate thousands of miles south from North America to spend the winter here."

"Are they real or 3-D butterflies?" asked Sailor.

"They look real," said Bryndis.

"I doubt it," said Emmett, stooping to inspect one that had landed on a fern next to him. "On the other hand..."

"I'm feeling much better now," said Renshaw. "Let's go."

Their energy renewed, the five of them continued hiking. Emmett took the lead and Cruz the rear. Not far beyond the sharp bend, a series of rock steps led to a clearing. Cruz froze on the final step. He'd never seen anything like this!

Thousands and thousands of monarch butterflies filled the air! Darting, zipping, swooping, gliding, the dainty insects danced among the explorers. So many gently beating wings reminded Cruz of the sound of raindrops. Clusters of resting butterflies covered the nearby pines and firs from top to bottom, weighing down the boughs and transforming the drab brown trunks into shimmering tangerine waves. Several monarchs lit on Cruz's arms, opening and closing their wings as they soaked up the sun. Cruz had to capture this!

Juggling his tablet so he didn't disturb the insects, Cruz tapped on his camera and turned it on his teammates. Dugan was standing on a rock. His hood up and his head hunched down between his shoulder blades, he looked uncomfortable—almost scared. Bryndis was working to rescue a butterfly that had crawled inside Renshaw's jacket. Emmett was gazing up, trying to see past a monarch that had mistaken his glowing fuchsia pink glasses for a flower. Sailor seemed to be having the most fun. She had her head back and her arms out, inviting the dainty creatures to land on her—and many did.

"Welcome, explorers!" A three-dimensional holo-video of Professor Gabriel appeared beside Cruz. "I am sure you're enjoying the wonder of these incredible insects, but this is a conservation training mission, after all. Gather 'round, please." The team huddled around the holo-video.

"By now you have probably figured out you are at the Monarch Butterfly Biosphere Reserve in El Santuario del Rosario, Michoacán, Mexico," said the faux Professor Gabriel. "Up to a billion butterflies from central and eastern Canada and the United States migrate here each fall to spend the winter in the oyamel fir forests. Some will jour-ney more than three thousand miles to reach this location."

Renshaw whistled under his breath.

"Monarchs are the only butterflies to migrate the way birds do, and we have much to learn about how and why they do so," said Professor Gabriel. "Your assignment is to record where some of these insects originated so we can learn more about their migration patterns." He explained that many of the butterflies had been tagged before setting off on their migration route. The explorers were to look for monarchs that were tagged with stickers attached to their wings, record the alphanumeric sequence, then go online and match the numbers to the original tagging location to see how far the butterfly had traveled.

"Log on to my website and you'll find instructions on how to properly hold a butterfly," said Professor Gabriel. "Please divide into teams of two. Each team will record the tags of twenty butterflies. Once you have completed your task, send your results to me. When all three teams have sent in their results, your mission will be complete and the simulation will end. Please remain in this clearing. Any questions?"

No one had any.

"Pair up and begin."

As the professor's image began to fade, the entire woodland landscape flickered. Cruz saw a flash of bare walls. It was only for a fraction of a second. "Did you see that?" he asked Emmett.

"No, what?"

"That flicker in the holo-video."

"Probably a power surge. Maybe a software glitch." Emmett gazed up. "Looks okay now."

Cruz glanced around. Emmett was right. Everything seemed fine.

Sailor clamped a hand on to Cruz's arm. "Hiya, partner."

Emmett looked disappointed, however, he quickly chose Bryndis as his partner. That left Renshaw stuck with Dugan. Cruz felt bad for Renshaw, but what could he do? Cruz promised himself that he'd pair up with Dugan next time. It was only fair.

Cruz and Sailor carefully picked their way to the far side of the

clearing to a log covered in resting monarchs. They spotted several butterflies with white stickers on their wings. Sailor read aloud Professor Gabriel's instructions on how to hold a butterfly. It seemed simple enough—grasp the insect gently by its closed wings, read and record the sequence on the tag, place the butterfly back where you found it.

"How about one person holds the butterfly and reads off the ID to the other person, who records it," said Sailor. "We can each do ten."

"Sounds good."

She nudged him. "You first."

"O-okay," said Cruz. He put out a hesitant hand. "If it's a real butterfly, I'm afraid I might rub off some scales and it won't be able to fly."

"That's a myth," said Sailor. "Butterflies can fly without scales. They can even fly with most of their wings broken or missing. It'll be okay."

Cruz found a butterfly whose wings were closed. He ever so gently closed his index finger and thumb around the top of its wings to hold it still. "Easy, buddy," he said. "This will only take a second."

"What does it feel like?" asked Sailor.

"Silk."

"Can you see the number?"

Leaning in, Cruz read out the sequence on the tag. Once Sailor confirmed the ID, Cruz released the insect. He let out a relieved sigh.

"According to the chart," said Sailor, "this butterfly came from Minnesota."

Cruz watched it unfold its wings, but he wasn't convinced he hadn't harmed it until he saw the butterfly take off. "One down, nine to go."

They finished Cruz's batch of butterflies and had two left in Sailor's group when a sharp *thump, thump, thump* shattered the peace of the forest.

"What was that?" said Sailor, her head swiveling.

"No idea."

They heard it again.

"It sounds like someone's chopping wood," said Sailor.

"It does, doesn't it?" Cruz tried to peer through the fir branches. He didn't see anything.

Thump, thump, thump.

"Maybe we should go see what it is," said Cruz.

"It's not part of the assignment." Sailor bent toward the butterfly in her hand. "LYR-047."

"They could be cutting down trees illegally or something."

"Remember Dr. Gabriel's instructions? We're supposed to stay here. Did you get that number?"

"Yeah. LYR-047. We shouldn't ignore it, Sailor, especially if someone is doing something wrong."

"I'm not sure it's a good idea to confront criminals."

"Who's confronting? Our textbook says conservationists are supposed to report things like poaching and illegal hunting and logging to the authorities," said Cruz. "I'll take a couple of pictures from a safe distance and turn them in to Professor Gabriel with our assignment. We'll be so quiet, they won't even know we're there."

"That's all?"

"That's all. We might even get bonus points."

Sailor's dark eyebrows went up. "We could use some bonus points after what happened last week. Okay, we can check it out, but let's not go very far."

"We won't."

They made their way through the brush in the direction of the chopping sound.

"Why don't we send up Mell to take the pictures?" asked Sailor from behind him.

"I didn't bring her," he called back. "And even if I had, I wouldn't want her flying around in the simulator. She could crash into a wall."

"Cruz, I think we should—"

Taking cover behind an oak, he held up a hand.

About 30 yards away, two big men were using axes to chop down a fir tree. Cruz quietly lifted his phone and began taking photos.

"Hurry," hissed Sailor, her hands on his shoulders.

"They don't have chainsaws like commercial loggers," whispered Cruz. "I bet they're from the local village. They're probably trying to get firewood for their families or wood to build a house."

"Whatever." Sailor lifted her phone. "Let's take our pics and get the heck out of here—"

Crack!

Cruz felt something whiz past his shoulder. He dropped to the ground.

"What was that?" squealed Sailor.

Cruz yanked her down with him. "*That* was a gunshot."

"Seriously? You mean they're shooting at us? They can't do that—"

"I think someone forgot to tell them that."

"What should we do?"

"*Go!*"

They took off through the woods. As he ran, branches smacked Cruz's legs and grabbed at his clothes. He could hear the men chasing them. Cruz could tell they were shouting in Spanish, though it was hard to hear. He caught a few words, like *niños,* which means "children," and *rápido,* which means "fast." The voices were getting louder. The men were gaining on them!

"Come on, Sailor, they're catching up!"

"Sorry!" She huffed. "If I'd known we were going to have to outrun some bad guys, I'd have worn my sneakers."

Cruz had lost the trail, but spotted an opening in the trees ahead of them. The clearing! If they could reach the group, maybe the men would give up the chase—

Was that mist? Cruz put on the brakes. He skidded to a stop inches from the edge of a cliff, then threw out an arm to keep Sailor from going over the side. She latched on to him and, for a moment, teetered on the edge before he could get his other arm around her to pull her back. Heaving, they watched the rocks she'd kicked disappear into the white spray of a raging waterfall.

"We're trapped!" cried Sailor.

Cruz looked back at the men, then into the canyon, then back at the men. "We've got to jump!" he shouted above the roar of the water.

"No." She vigorously shook her head. "No way am I—"

"We have no choice."

"Are you kidding? It's got to be a ninety-meter drop. We'll die."

"We might survive the fall," he yelled. "We won't survive the gunshots."

"I can't believe this is happening."

Cruz gave her a wry grin. "It's not, you know."

She scowled at him. "Next time, dibs on Emmett."

"Fair enough." He flung a hand out to Sailor. "Ready?"

Sailor grabbed his hand. She held on so tight, Cruz thought she might snap his knuckles. "Ready."

"We'll go on the count of three," he yelled. "One . . . two . . . three!"

They jumped.

Sailor closed her eyes. Cruz didn't.

10

CRUZ stared, unblinking, at the wall of screens in their classroom. It was strange to see a video of himself plunging through the mist of a 300-foot waterfall like a stuntman in an action movie. Except it wasn't a movie. And it wasn't real life. It was sort of something between the two, which was completely weird. The video faded to black before Cruz and Sailor hit the river, or so the story would have gone *had* they been in a movie. In the simulator, however, the pair had dropped only about 15 feet before landing on a huge inflatable cushion. When they rolled off the bag, they found themselves back in a section of the large room they'd seen on their first day in the CAVE. There was no blue sky. No forest. No butterflies. For them, the mission was finished. Cruz had been disappointed. He'd hoped they would really splash down into water!

That was only yesterday, though it seemed like an eternity ago.

"Let's review." Professor Gabriel stepped to the front of the classroom, his bald head glowing under the lights. "What might Cruz and Sailor have done differently in this scenario?"

Dugan snorted. "You mean other than die?"

Everyone laughed.

Cruz slid down in his seat. Next to him, Sailor had her hand over her eyes.

Ekaterina Pajarin raised a hand. "They should have followed your instructions to stay in the clearing."

"Good." Professor Gabriel pointed to Matteo Montefiore, who had his hand up.

"Or if they did need to leave, they should have told other team members where they were going and when they would be back," said Matteo.

"Right. Anyone else?" asked their instructor.

"Once they saw the illegal logging going on, they should not have stuck around to take photos," said Zane. "That was risky. They should have hurried back to the clearing or gotten to a safe location where they could call the authorities."

"Correct," said Professor Gabriel.

"So much for *fortes fortuna adiuvat*," Cruz mumbled to Sailor, who still had her eyes covered. She was slumped down so far her head was hitting the back of her seat.

Emmett and Bryndis had gotten a perfect score of 100 points on their portion of the training mission. Renshaw and Dugan had come in six points behind. They had misread the numbers on two tags and had lost count and done only 19 of their 20 insect IDs, although by the way Renshaw had moped, you'd have thought he'd completely failed. Cruz and Sailor had lost two points for not completing the last of Sailor's butterflies and another 20 points for not surviving. They'd earned 78 points out of 100. Ugh. Cruz wouldn't blame Sailor if she never spoke to him again.

Professor Gabriel approached Cruz and Sailor. *Here it comes!* Cruz planted both feet squarely on the floor. He sat up as tall as he could. He was braced and ready for a lecture.

"Did you make some errors in judgment?" Dr. Gabriel's scraggly eyebrows went up. "Yes. Could your actions have gotten you seriously injured, if not killed? Most certainly. Would I ever recommend doing what you did? Absolutely not."

Cruz felt himself shrinking. He grabbed on to the sides of his chair to keep from sliding down any farther.

Professor Gabriel stroked his chin. "And yet . . ."

Cruz's ears went up. It was remarkable how such a little word could hold so much hope.

Sailor was peeking between her fingers.

"You were the only two explorers in your entire class to even acknowledge the chopping noise you heard in the forest," said their teacher. "An explorer must always be aware of his or her surroundings, and, when the situation calls for it, be willing to get involved." Professor Gabriel came to stand behind Cruz and Sailor. "Bravo to you for being willing to stick your necks out. You wanted to make a difference, and that should be the ultimate goal for every explorer. In light of this, Cruz and Sailor, for this mission, I'm awarding you ten bonus points."

Locking eyes, Cruz's and Sailor's jaws dropped. They were both thinking the same thing: The extra points meant they were only 12 points behind Emmett and Bryndis! And in the rankings, that put them in seventh place out of twelve pairs for this mission. Not perfect, but not a total catastrophe, either.

"All right, class, that was the last CAVE video," said Dr. Gabriel. "Please take out your tablets and bring up chapter four, on habitat conservation."

As everyone dug into their backpacks, Professor Gabriel bent between Cruz and Sailor. "Fortune may favor the brave," he said softly, "but the wise endure. Understand?"

Cruz and Sailor nodded solemnly.

"Thought I'd seen it all in twenty-three years of teaching." Professor Gabriel chuckled. "No one ever jumped into the falls before."

"**F**INALLY!" SAID LANI, over the buzz of her school cafeteria. It was lunchtime back home. "I've been trying to reach you forever."

"We would have been here sooner, but the Bottomless Pit had thirds for dinner," said Cruz, scooting back on his bed.

"Thirds?"

"He ate an entire whale!"

"Salmon," said Emmett. He was firing up his computers. "It was salmon."

"We could use some salmon here," said Lani, waving around a limp leaf of lettuce on her fork. She stuck her face close to the camera. "Lunch is almost over, so I'd better tell you what I found out."

Cruz felt the hair on the back of his neck stand up.

"Hold on." She dug her notebook out of her backpack. "Okay, there are fewer than a hundred people in the U.S. with the last name Nebula. As far as I could find, none are in the Washington, D.C., area. Unfortunately, Nebula *is* a popular name among companies. I've got a list of about twenty-five businesses and organizations with the name in their titles, everything from a book publisher to a cat shelter to a company that makes cold and flu medicines."

"Oh yeah," said Emmett. "I've taken Nebula cough syrup before."

"I'll send you the full list," said Lani. "Do you want me to keep searching?"

"No," said Cruz. "It sounds like I'll need to narrow things down from my end. I've been a little busy—"

"That's right. How did your training mission go?"

Cruz tried to keep his face expressionless. "It went great. Just great."

"Uh-oh. What happened?"

How does *she do that?* "We sort of . . . died."

"*What?*"

"Sailor and I jumped off a cliff."

"I repeat: You *WHAT?*"

"It's a long story," Cruz replied sheepishly.

"Theoretically, it is possible you could have survived the fall, since you landed in water," called Emmett.

"Thank you," said Cruz. "I would have said that to Professor Gabriel, but I was afraid he would take away our ten bonus points for spotting the illegal loggers."

"Are you guys going to fill me in here?" demanded Lani. "I'm talking to you, so clearly you're not dead. But you jumped off a cliff?"

Cruz was ready to move on to a new topic, but Emmett chimed in again.

"He had no choice, he was being shot at."

"*WHAT?* What kind of school is this?!" Lani screeched.

"It was just a training mission. Simulation thing," Cruz explained, giving as little detail as possible. He'd made a vow to Dr. Hightower not to reveal the technology behind how the CAVE worked, and he didn't want to slip up. He would give Lani the full story later, but slowly and carefully and without revealing any vital CAVE secrets.

"Fine, Mr. Mysterious. Be that way." Lani's fake pout turned to a smile. "So, boss, what's my next assignment?"

Cruz noticed the mailbox icon at the top of his tablet was blinking. It was a message from Aunt Marisol: *Need to see you. Come by my office tonight. I'll be here until nine.* No doubt, she had heard about his tragic end in the CAVE and had plenty to say on the subject.

"Cruz?" Lani was waiting.

"Uh … nothing, for now. Thanks for your help."

"What are you going to—" The lunch bell interrupted her. Lani tossed her napkin on her tray. "Do me a favor? Take Mell with you wherever you go from now on."

"Lani, I don't need—"

"Do I have to get on a plane and come all the way to Washington, D.C.?"

"Fine, I'll take Mell."

"Turn your tablet toward Emmett." When Cruz did, Lani said, "Emmett, please watch out for Cruz. I know him. He's going to try to be some kind of a hero and end up getting hurt. Or worse."

"Don't worry, Lani. I'm on it," said Emmett without turning around. He was studying blueprints laid out on all three of his computer screens.

"What is that?" Lani mouthed to Cruz.

He lifted a shoulder. "He'll tell me when he's ready." With a wave to his best friend, Cruz logged off. He reached for Mell and dropped the drone into the pocket of his coat. "Be back in an hour or so," he said, slipping his arms into the sleeves.

Emmett was still glued to his screens. "Where are you going?"

Cruz didn't want to tell his roommate he was about to get in trouble with his aunt. "To ... uh ... the library."

"Wearing your coat?"

"Um ... yeah ... it's cold in there." He winced. It wasn't even a good lie.

"True," said his roommate, to his surprise. "The ideal temperature at which books should be stored is between sixty and sixty-four degrees Fahrenheit with an approximate relative humidity of fifty percent. I suspect Mr. Rook keeps the temperature around sixty-six degrees, which is acceptable for humans but still chilly, especially for those from a tropical climate, like Hawaii. Before you come back, will you do me a favor and ask Mr. Rook exactly what temperature he keeps the library?"

"Uh-huh."

"Ask him if the ideal climate in the special collections room is different from the main library?"

"Yeah. Sure."

"And if it *is* different, what's the diff—"

"Okay, okay!" Cruz threw up his hands. "I'm not going to the library. The truth is, Aunt Marisol asked to see me. She's probably going to ream me about our CAVE disaster yesterday. Satisfied?"

Emmett bit his lip. "Sorry."

"Cruz?" Renshaw popped his head into their room. "Can I borrow your biology notes from today? I think I missed something on analyzing biomes. Dr. Ishikawa always talks so fast."

"Uh ... sure. I'll email them to you."

"Thanks."

"That's the third time this week Renshaw has asked for your notes," hissed Emmett once Renshaw had left.

"I don't mind." Cruz shrugged. "He's just a perfectionist."

"You say that like it's a good thing."

"Isn't it?"

"Hardly. Nothing's ever good enough for a perfectionist. If they get an A they're unhappy. They want to know why they didn't get an A plus."

"What if they get an A plus?"

"They want an A plus plus. And if they get an A plus plus, they'll squeeze out every last extra credit point they possibly can. Trust me, I used to be one of *them*."

Cruz looked at Emmett's row of computers. "You're not anymore?"

"Nope. Now I'm a semi-perfectionist, which is much better. Only half of me strives for perfection; the other half just wants to sleep late."

Cruz laughed. "I gotta go. See you later. Don't work too hard." As he crossed the courtyard between the Academy and the administration building, Cruz paused to watch the last remnants of the sun fade behind the trees. The sky was turning a deep violet. A quick check of his tablet showed he had a message. It was from Renshaw. He'd attached a cute chipmunk icon with instructions for Cruz to click on it. When Cruz did, the chipmunk did a little dance and held up a sign that said THANK YOU.

Snickering, Cruz held his Open Sesame band up to the security camera next to the door of the administration building. Inside, only a few overhead lights were on. Cruz took the stairs two at a time to the second floor. The place was deserted. He poked his head around the open door of his aunt's office. She was sitting at her desk. Under the glow of a thin lamp with a curved stem, she was typing on her laptop. "Hi, Aunt Marisol," he said quietly, so he wouldn't startle her, but she jumped anyway.

"Cruz! Come in and have a seat. Close the door, please."

Uh-oh. If she wanted him to shut the door, it meant a lecture was coming. To the right was a glass cabinet filled with artifacts from her many travels: clay sculptures, stone tools, feather masks, and metal jewelry. The wall to his left was a massive bookcase, its shelves sagging with anthropology books. On the top shelf, a bronze elephant clock did double duty as a bookend. An oak closet took most of the right wall. Cruz couldn't help wondering: If he opened the thick doors, would he find himself in Narnia? He sat in one of the two wood chairs with blue-and-green-plaid cushions angled toward the desk. Everything was in a neat row on the antique oak desk. His eyes traveled over a stack of folders, a clear plastic square of paper clips, and a framed photo of Cruz and his dad standing in front of their surf shop.

"I know what you're going to say," said Cruz. "I am so sorry." He couldn't believe he was having to apologize *again.* Even he was getting tired of hearing himself say it.

"Sorry? For ...?" Her brow was furrowed. It was a miracle! Aunt Marisol hadn't heard about the disaster in the CAVE. *Thank you, Professor Gabriel!*

"Uh ... nothing."

One eyebrow went up. "Please tell me you got to your training mission on time."

"I did. I was even early." He reached forward to touch a honey brown sandstone statue of a flat-headed skull with no eyes. Its edges were round and worn, as if it had been relentlessly pounded by the ocean surf for centuries.

"It's a zemi, a Taíno religious relic," explained Aunt Marisol. "The Taíno were a Caribbean culture. They were the first indigenous people in the Western Hemisphere to greet Spanish explorers."

"You mean they met Christopher Columbus?"

"Yes. He was quite taken with them—said they were a generous and giving people and would make good servants." She sighed. "Back then, 'explorer' tended to be just another word for 'conqueror.' If the explorers didn't wipe out a culture with their weapons, you can bet their diseases did."

"Like when the Spanish conquered the Aztec," said Cruz, citing their own ancestral Mexican heritage.

"Precisely. Thank goodness today's explorers are much different."

Cruz took his hand from the zemi. "So what's up?"

Scooting her chair back almost to the wall of windows behind her, Aunt Marisol stood up. "I have something for you." Unlocking one of the arched doors of the oak closet, his aunt went on tiptoe to reach the top shelf. She took down an aqua blue box a bit bigger than a package of Oreos. Aunt Marisol blew dust off the box before placing it on the desk between them. She set it down so carefully Cruz wondered if it contained explosives.

"When we talked in the courtyard," she said, "and you asked about your mother, I wasn't sure if I should show this to you. I worried it might make things worse, but then I thought, it won't be long before we set sail on *Orion*. And if I don't do it now, then when?"

"Do what?"

"After the accident, they . . . someone . . . cleaned out her desk," explained his aunt. "Your mom's personal things from her office are . . . they're in here."

In one motion, Cruz slid his chair back as far from her desk as possible. Wood scraping against wood made an earsplitting shriek, sending a tsunami of goose bumps up his spine.

"I'm sorry." Aunt Marisol lunged for the box. "I shouldn't have—"

"Wait," cried Cruz. "You surprised me, that's all."

She straightened, clasping her hands against her heart. For a

minute or two, they did nothing but stare at the box and listen to the elephant clock tick.

"So what's in it?" Cruz's voice was barely above a whisper.

"I don't know. I've never opened it."

"Never?"

"I almost did. Once. But no."

Cruz stood up. He moved toward her desk. He felt like a feather in the wind, light and breathless and adrift, in control of nothing. Trying to keep his hands steady, Cruz lifted the lid.

His heart skipped a beat.

As the lid parted from its box, Cruz saw some assorted pens and pencils. There was a pad of cat-shaped sticky notes, a tiny bag of almonds, and a box of bandages. Sifting through the contents, Cruz stopped to inspect a smooth metal disk with a hole in the middle. It appeared to be a washer, the kind you use with nuts and bolts to keep from damaging whatever it is you're screwing the bolt into. There was a ridged washer in the box, too. As his fingers skimmed the bottom, they closed around a tiny silver object. Cruz picked it up. It was a min-iature Aztec crown. At the tip of the crown was a small hook. It must have once been on a charm bracelet—*her* charm bracelet?

Was it possible to be relieved and disappointed at the same time? Cruz was glad the box held no horrible revelations, yet he was no closer to learning the truth about what had happened to his mother.

In the corner of the box was a simple key—one that might go to a jewelry box or a suitcase. Beneath the key was an old photograph. Sliding the picture free, Cruz found himself staring at the familiar face of a young boy. The image was of him. It was summer and he was on a kiddie ride at an amusement park, strapped inside one of the colorful fish cars that went up and down and around in

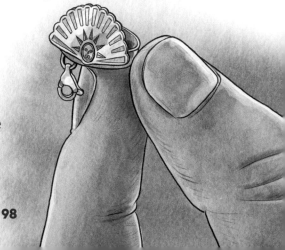

a circle. He was laughing as he passed the camera. Cruz couldn't remember ever being on such a ride.

That was the worst part. The few memories he had of his mother were bits and pieces—swinging at the playground or riding in the car or skipping down a trail. Snippets here and there, but nothing complete. Nothing whole. If not for the beach holo-video, Cruz wouldn't have even been able to recall the sound of her voice.

It wasn't fair. Her death had not been anything like they had been led to believe. She hadn't been in the wrong place at the wrong time. There had been no heroics. No scientific breakthroughs. No glory. She had been taken from them—cruelly and deliberately. He felt a stew of sadness, frustration, helplessness, and rage brewing within him. The photograph crumbled in his grip.

Aunt Marisol was beside him. "Don't torture yourself. Your mom wouldn't want that. We have to be satisfied with—"

He held his hand up between them. He didn't want to hear any more. He didn't want to be coddled or lied to or even comforted. And he certainly did not want to be satisfied. Cruz wasn't satisfied and never would be, because the only thing he wanted he could not have.

He put the lid back on the box, picked it up, and tucked it under his arm. "I'd better go. I've got a lot of homework."

"If you need to talk—"

"I know. I'll ... I'll be okay. Thanks, Aunt Marisol ... for this." Crossing the courtyard, Cruz did not need to turn around to know she was watching from her window—watching the way a mother would. He had always longed to let her be that to him, and now, here at the Academy, he wished for it more than ever. But if whoever was behind Nebula knew how close the two of them were, they might try to hurt her, too. Cruz couldn't let that happen. He had already lost one mother. He could not bear to lose another.

11

MARYLAND

MARYLAND

Washington,
D.C.

ROCK CREEK PARK,
WASHINGTON,
D.C.

VIRGINIA

Potomac

Anacostia

MARYLAND

"DOESN'T *anybody* know where we're going?"

asked Tao Sun, nervously twisting the end of a black pigtail.

"Just our driver, and he's not talking," Sailor, who was sitting behind the driver, said with a sigh. Unable to coax him into giving up any info, she'd flopped back into her seat.

Earlier that morning, the explorers had received a mysterious message from their fitness and survival training instructor:

> *Dear Explorers,*
> *Our regularly scheduled fitness/survival*
> *training class at 10 a.m. has been rescheduled*
> *for this evening. Please assemble in the*
> *Academy lobby at 7 p.m. Wear your regular*
> *workout gear and sneakers. Bring a jacket*
> *and water.*
> > *L'aventure vous attend!*
> > *M. Legrand*

Seth Moller, an explorer from Luxembourg, told them *l'aventure vous attend* means "adventure awaits you," so not much of a hint there. And it was Taryn, not Monsieur Legrand, who'd met them in the lobby. Ushering them out the front door to a pair of vans parked at the curb, all she would say was, "Your instructor is waiting for you at your destination." She gave them a wink. "Enjoy!"

Monsieur Romain Legrand was one of Cruz's favorite teachers. Cruz loved hearing about his outdoor adventures, and it didn't take much convincing to get the Frenchman to recount his harrowing experiences climbing K2 (he had almost died of altitude sickness), trekking across the Atacama Desert (he had almost died of desert fever), and cave diving in the Yucatán cenotes (he had almost died of the bends). Oh, and he was once an aerial performer with Cirque du Soleil (he had almost died when a ribbon snapped).

Cruz figured Monsieur Legrand probably had something risky up his sleeve. But what? He glanced out the window at the colonial-style brick homes rolling past. The sun was beginning to dip behind the trees as they turned off the main road. A mile or so later, Cruz saw a DEER CROSSING sign, soon followed by another sign: ROCK CREEK PARK.

Everyone suddenly began talking.

"I bet they're going to drop us off in the middle of the forest and we'll have to find our way out," said Renshaw.

"You mean we're going to be here all night?" groaned Dugan.

"Well, it is called fitness and *survival* training," said Emmett. "I guess this is the survival part."

"We'll have to live off the land," said Zane.

"That better not mean eating any bugs," gulped Sailor. "I'm a vegetarian."

Cruz chuckled. Less than two hours ago, he'd seen the girl cut into a hunk of meatloaf. "Since when?"

"Since now."

The vans snaked through several miles of thick forest, then turned off the two-lane road onto a rocky dirt path. They rumbled over bumpy gravel for another five minutes before coming to a stop near an old railroad tunnel. Cruz was the first to jump out of his van. Clouds obscured the stars. The only light in the area came from the other end of the abandoned train tunnel about 60 yards away. As they walked through the round passage made of stacked river rocks, Bryndis glanced around. "Not crazy about this."

Cruz was beginning to feel on edge, too. He felt a chilly wind on his shoulders. Goose bumps twizzled up his arms and neck. He could hear water dripping.

When they emerged from the tunnel, Cruz shielded his eyes against dozens of bright lights. At first, he thought it must be a stadium, but then he realized they were in an open field. Spread out before them were various pieces of equipment: hurdles, monkey bars, a cargo net, and a real rock wall.

"It's an obstacle course!" cried Cruz, relaxing. "This is gonna be fun."

"Yeah. Fun," said Emmett flatly.

The course was surrounded by an assortment of computer screens, speakers, and projectors on tripods.

A tanned, lean man in his mid-30s with deep-set blue eyes and shoulder-length streaked brown hair stood at the edge of the course. "Welcome to Rock Creek Park!" said Monsieur Legrand. "You are probably surprised to find such a large park not far from the Academy. It covers more than seventeen hundred acres, so we should not be disturbed in our hidden meadow. The park has a zoo, a planetarium, a horse center, and even a few secrets. The most intrepid explorers can find piles of stones here that were once part of the original Capitol Building. However, tonight you will not be exploring. You will be competing in what we call the Augmented Reality Challenge, or ARC. It's a real obstacle course with a few virtual surprises thrown in."

There was a chorus of excited gasps.

"Jovan?" Their fitness instructor motioned for an older boy to come and stand next to him. Cruz knew the boy right away. He'd never forget Big Deal—the kid who'd hassled him in the lobby that first day.

Jovan spotted Cruz, too. "Hey, California surfer dude!" he called like they were close friends.

Cruz raised a hand, then quickly dropped it.

"You know my brother?" Renshaw was beside Cruz.

"*That's* your brother?"

"Aye."

Monsieur Legrand began explaining how the game worked. "You'll each put on a set of elbow and knee pads and a helmet. As you navigate the course, a computer inside the helmet will generate virtual elements. It will be your task to complete all the obstacles, handling whatever real and virtual challenges come your way. Fall or fail to do one, and you're out. Whoever clocks the fastest time wins."

"Where's the finish line?" asked Zane.

"The rock wall," answered their teacher. "Once you get over the top, the chip in your helmet will stop the clock."

"Don't be upset if you don't make it through the course," added Jovan. "Few first-year recruits do." He adjusted his elbow pads and pulled on a shiny black helmet emblazoned with a yellow *A*. Giving them the thumbs up, Jovan jogged to the start line.

Monsieur Legrand motioned to the large screens mounted at each end of the course. "The helmets' computers are connected to the screens so we'll be able to see exactly what you are seeing as you move through each challenge. Jovan will do a few obstacles to give you an idea of what you can expect, but don't form your strategy based on his experience. Each run will offer different virtual components."

Jovan flipped the visor down over his eyes. "Ready," he said, his voice crackling from the speakers behind them. Cruz made a note to remember there was a mic in the helmet. The explorers turned their eyes to the screen closest to them. The picture also included a clock in the lower corner so they could keep track of Jovan's time. Monsieur Legrand put the whistle to his lips.

When he heard the *thweet,* Jovan hit the start line, tripping the digital timer. They watched him charge toward the first obstacle, a straightaway of six hurdles. He glided gazelle-like over the first five bars. As he approached the final hurdle, something appeared in his viewer. It was a crystal goblet! The glass was precariously perched on top of the right side of the hurdle. Jovan had only a second to correct for it before taking the jump. As he went over, his knee nicked the hurdle. Cruz and the rest of the explorers let out a collective gasp. The glass wobbled, spilling a bit of water, but did not fall. Jovan hurried to the next station, the monkey bars; but these were no ordinary bars. The sides were curved, not only from side to side, but up and down, too, making the whole thing look like it was melting. Jovan scampered up the ladder. Grabbing the first bar, he swung out to catch the next one and moved swiftly from bar to bar: left and up, right and down, left and down farther still, right and back up again. Cruz was impressed with his upper-body strength and agility. Jovan had made it about halfway across when his viewer showed something flying toward him. Bats! Unsure if they were real or virtual, Cruz let out a shiver. Jovan didn't panic. He lowered his helmet and hung on with both hands until the last bat had flown past. He swung his body a few times to get his momentum going again and made it to the platform on the other side. Monsieur Legrand blew his whistle. Everyone clapped.

Cruz got it. The virtual elements were distractions. Ignore them, keep calm, keep going, and you'd do okay.

"Thank you, Jovan." Monsieur Legrand looked to his students. "Now it's your turn. Oh, there's one more thing."

"Wuh-oh," Emmett muttered to Cruz. "Here it comes."

"You will not only be racing against the clock," said their instructor, "but you will be racing against each other. You will do the obstacle course in pairs."

Emmett and Cruz stood together to indicate they were a team, but Monsieur Legrand had other ideas. He held up a small black velvet bag. "In here are two sets of numbers from one to twelve. Pick a number, find the person with the corresponding number, and that's who you'll be racing against." Cruz stifled a moan.

Cruz hoped he picked a high number. He preferred to watch how the other explorers handled the course first. Cruz dipped his hand into the bag and felt several wood chips. He grabbed one, then at the last second exchanged it for another. Pulling his hand out, Cruz opened his palm. The round chip had the number two on it. *Rats!* People began pairing up. Emmett and Zane. Renshaw and Sailor. Ali and Bryndis. Ekaterina and Tao. Soon, only one person besides Cruz stood alone: Dugan. He held up his chip. It had a numeral two on it. This time, Cruz did moan aloud.

Renshaw and Sailor were first. As they lined up at the start, the picture on the large screen split so the explorers could see a side-by-side view from both competitors' helmets. Monsieur Legrand blew the whistle and Sailor and Renshaw were off. Over the first three hurdles, they were neck and neck. Sailor took the lead when Renshaw tapped his toe on the fourth bar. It did not topple. As they bounded to the fifth, a gust of wind blasted them from the left side. Bits of sand and rock almost completely obscured their vision. Renshaw crashed into the hurdle. He was out. Sailor stumbled, but recovered and made it over the last two hurdles.

She climbed the ladder to the monkey bars. Leaping from the platform, she grabbed the first bar and swung to the second bar, then down to the third, the lowest bar on the apparatus. "I hear something," she said. Her helmet tipped down to reveal a pit of hot, bubbling lava licking her toes. "*Arrgh!*" Sailor shrieked, her swing slowing. She kicked her legs out and shifted her grip. She was in trouble.

"Come on, Sailor, fight!" Cruz tried to will her forward.

"Bloody lava," they heard a second before Sailor fell to the cushioned bag below.

Stalking back to the group, Renshaw ripped off his helmet. "I can't believe I tanked on the first obstacle. The first one!"

"Nice try, Renshaw," said Monsieur Legrand. "*Bon travail.*"

"Good effort." Jovan slapped his brother on the back. "But sadly, not good enough."

Monsieur Legrand was calling for the next pair of competitors to get into position.

That was Cruz and Dugan. On his way to the starting line, Cruz got a good look at the course. Hurdles. Wavy monkey bars. Horizontal cargo net. Tunnel. Pond. Rock wall.

They passed Sailor on her way back to the group. Dugan snorted. "Way to blow chunks, York."

A fuming Sailor locked eyes with Cruz. She gritted her teeth. "Get 'im."

He lifted his palm. She slapped it. Hard. Cruz eased his helmet down over his ears and took his mark.

"Better enjoy the view now, Coronado," spit Dugan. "'Cause in a minute all you're gonna see is my dust."

"You wish." Giving Dugan his best game face, Cruz popped his visor down. He put his toes on the line, took two deep breaths, and gave himself a quick pep talk. *Focus. Keep calm. Go fast.*

Thweet!

Cruz shot out of the start. Pumping his arms as he raced toward the hurdles, he kept his eyes forward. He flew easily over the first three hurdles. On his way to the fourth, he saw something to his left. It was moving. Were those polka dots? Cruz turned his neck slightly. "Whoa!"

It was a cheetah! The sleek gold cat with dark spots easily paced him. The animal wasn't attempting to attack. He was simply running alongside, as if Cruz were another cat and the two were bounding through the tall grasses of the African savanna. Unable to break his gaze, Cruz smacked the final hurdle with his foot. The metal bar didn't

topple, but watching the big cat had cost Cruz valuable time. Dugan was now in the lead. *Dang!*

His competitor already scaling the ladder to the monkey bars, Cruz charged after him. He was only a few seconds behind.

If he could keep up, his best chance of passing Dugan was on the cargo net. With Dugan two bars ahead of him, Cruz swung out onto the first of eight bars. He moved like a pendulum, catching each bar almost as quickly as Dugan released it. His shoulders were starting to burn. His body felt heavy.

Boom! Was that a thunderclap? It began to rain. Hard. Torrents of water ran down the front of Cruz's helmet, blinding him. As he caught the seventh bar, his fingers slipped. With a grunt, he clamped down on the metal and forced his hips forward. He knew if he stopped swinging he was doomed. Just. One. More. Bar. He only had one more to go. Gritting his teeth, Cruz summoned as much energy as he could and flung himself forward. His foot caught metal. He let go, falling to his knees on the platform.

His visor cleared just in time for him to spot Dugan leaping onto the horizontal cargo net. Cruz followed, crawling across the net like a spider whose web has just ensnared a fly. He was making up time, too, when a virtual man in a safari hat leaned over the left side of the net. Holding a large hunting knife, the man began cutting the net away from its supports! Dugan had seen him, too, and was scrambling for the right corner. Cruz knew he had to go that way, too, if he hoped to reach the other side before the man cut the net free, but moving diagonally would mean he wouldn't be able to pass Dugan. Cruz pushed himself to go faster. He felt the rope slice the skin on his fingers and palms. His foot slipped on the netting, and he nearly fell through a space. As the man's knife sawed away at the last loop, Cruz jumped onto the scaffolding. Another close call, but he'd made it!

Scooting over the side, Cruz dropped to the ground and followed Dugan, who was just heading into the tunnel. Cruz had to bend forward going into the circular passage to keep from smacking his head. Within seconds of entering the dark, narrow tunnel, Cruz's nostrils were on fire. It smelled like rotten eggs. *Was that Dugan? Ew!* Cruz's first instinct was to hold his breath, but he knew that was a mistake. He needed full lung power. Ahead, Dugan had slowed. He was coughing.

By the time they came out of the tunnel, Cruz was on Dugan's heels. If he was going to pass he had to do it now!

Cruz made his move. As he came up on his left, Dugan threw out an elbow to block him. He was too late. Cruz whipped in front of him and took the lead. He raced to the pond, leaping onto the lily pad closest to shore. He hopped easily from pad to pad.

He was making good time and was two-thirds of the way across when he saw the dark green scales ripple. An alligator rose from the murky swamp, its massive jaws opening. Cruz saw teeth glisten in the light—huge, sharp teeth. The terrifying sight was enough to send him skidding to the edge of the lily pad. He couldn't stop. He was going in the water—real water! Cruz threw out his arms in a last-ditch effort to save himself, teetered for a second, then somehow, miraculously, his body stopped moving. He leaped over the last two pads and onto shore. Dugan was two steps behind him as they neared the final obstacle: the 30-foot rock wall.

Jovan was waiting at the base to give them instructions for getting into their safety harnesses, but Cruz didn't need any help. He'd taken a climbing class with his dad last year. He stepped into the harness, pulled it up to his waist, and adjusted the belt. He grabbed one of the ropes hanging from the wall and clipped it to his harness. Glancing up, Cruz took a few seconds to assess the situation. Experience told him it was important to first choose a route, a zigzag path of grips that would take him quickly and easily to the top. If he didn't, he could end up stuck under an outcrop and have to drop to the bottom and start all over again. Dugan was not as cautious. He was already climbing. Cruz put his foot on the first grip, reached out for one above his head, and pulled himself up onto the wall. He tried to move steadily up the jagged face, but the higher he scaled the farther apart the grips were. Plus, it had been a while since he'd climbed. His arms aching, his fingers bleeding, Cruz had to stop and rest more than once.

Meanwhile, Dugan was about eight feet above him. *How did he get up there so fast? What was he, part monkey?* Cruz knew if he didn't pick it up, Dugan was going to beat him. *Come on, come on!* Cruz stretched for a grip a fraction of an inch beyond his fingertips. *Just . . . a little . . . more . . .*

He felt a tremor. Then another. Cruz looked up. A wave of gravel and rocks was tumbling down. He hugged the wall as a torrent of stones, boulders, and debris fell around him. Fifteen seconds later, the rock-slide was over. Determined to finish, Cruz reached for the next grip. He didn't look down. He didn't look up. He stopped worrying about where Dugan was. He kept climbing, kept searching for the next grip and the next and the next until, at last, Cruz dived onto the top of the rock wall. He was on his back and every single muscle was screaming in pain, but he'd done it! He had made it through the obstacle course.

Helmet still on, Cruz flipped up his visor. Above him, the clouds had parted, revealing a pale yellow full moon.

Cruz sat up, still gasping. He looked for Dugan, ready to congratulate him on the win, but his opponent wasn't there. Cruz peered over the edge. Dugan was dangling from his rope near the base of the wall and scowling, his face redder than a fresh strawberry.

So if Dugan was down there, that meant . . .

"*Wooo-hooo!*" Cruz thrust his arms overhead. He had won!

From his perch, Cruz could see all the way across the meadow. His classmates were waving and cheering. Clinging to each other, Emmett and Sailor were wildly jumping. In his ear came Monsieur Legrand's smooth radio voice with a French accent. "Excellent, Cruz. Excellent!"

12

". . . SO FROM your reading, you've learned anthropology is the study of the characteristics of humanity—why different cultures, eat, speak, dress, think, believe, live, and act the way they do." Aunt Marisol's voice floated to Cruz from behind him. She liked to roam as she lectured, and her calm voice was enough to lull him to sleep on this Tuesday morning. Cruz put a hand to his mouth to hide a yawn.

"On our global travels, you'll explore tombs, caves, ruins, and other ancient structures to learn about societies of the past," continued his aunt, "but you will also do more—much more." As she came around his right side, Cruz looked up into dark, sparkling eyes. "You will get to experience life in the *present* in these regions. You'll eat the food of the native people, sing their songs, wear their clothes, join in their celebrations, hear their legends and lore, and discover what makes them unique. I encourage you not to shy away from these opportunities but to embrace them. They are extraordinary and you may never get to do them again."

Cruz realized he was leaning forward in his seat. So was everyone else. The room was still, the air thick with possibilities.

His aunt smiled. "Guess I got a bit carried away, huh?" Red high-heeled sandals strolled to the front of the class. Turning to face them, she straightened the hem of her matching blazer. "What are the four subfields of anthropology, please?"

Cruz flung his hand in the air, as did 23 other explorers.

"Zane?"

"Biological, cultural, linguistic, and archaeological."

"Thank you. For your next assignment, students, I want each of you to choose one of these subfields and create a one-minute holo-video commercial. It should be like a real ad, designed to entice young people to enter the profession. Explain what anthropologists study in the discipline you've selected, give examples of what they have discovered, and explain how the world is better for it. Mr. Rook and his library staff are ready to assist you with equipment and visual aids. Also, remember your third CAVE mission is an archaeological dig in South America, so be sure to read chapters five through seven in your text. We'll talk more about that next week..."

"I can't wait to go on our first dig," Cruz whispered to Emmett.

"Same here."

"I can't believe how fast it's going. Do you realize we're already halfway through our training? In two weeks, we'll be on the ship for real!"

"Two weeks?" A shadow crossed Emmett's face. "Wow, that is so great!" he said, quickly recovering. It was too late. Cruz had seen the truth, and the truth was that something was bothering Emmett.

CRUZ SMILED A SATISFIED SMILE. He had already done a lot of work on his anthropology holo-video ad Aunt Marisol had assigned the class that morning. It was going to be terrific, if he did say so himself. He had chosen archaeology as his subfield and was going to do a commercial as if he were inside King Tut's tomb, showing all of its relics and treasures. Mr. Rook had helped him find some incredible three-dimensional images of artifacts to share, including the boy king's solid gold sarcophagus, the famous gold-and-lapis burial mask, and several pieces of ornate gold jewelry. "Thanks for all your help, Mr. Rook," Cruz had said to the librarian. "I think Aunt Ma—

I mean, Dr. Coronado—is going to love this."

"My pleasure!" He'd grinned. "That's what I'm here for. Fingers crossed you get an A. Let me know how it goes, okay?"

"I will."

"Cruz?" Emmett was at the window now.

Cruz was trying to hit the perfect edit point on his video and wasn't really listening. "Uh-huh?"

"There's a guy standing under the awning of the coffee shop across the street."

"Uh-huh."

"He's wearing black snakeskin cowboy boots."

In a flash, Cruz was beside him. The man was sheltered under the green-and-red-striped awning directly opposite their end of the Academy. They could only see him from the waist down. The boys watched people go in and out of the coffee shop and up and down the street.

The man didn't seem to be doing anything. Just standing, facing the school. Everyone was in motion around the guy, who remained rooted to the cement. Finally, after several minutes, he stepped forward out of the shadows of the awning. A dark head tipped back, and for the first time Cruz saw his face. Cruz had expected him to be a sinister sort with at least one creepy feature (besides the boots), like a hairy mole, a black eye patch, or a neck tattoo. But he didn't have any of those things. With a head full of dark wavy hair, a stubbled chin, and a leather jacket, he looked like a model. Add a scarf and he could have starred in a luxury car commercial.

"That's him!" Emmett's voice went up an octave. "That's the guy from the airport."

Goose bumps tripping down his arms, Cruz hopped backward. Emmett did the same. Now the roommates stood perfectly still a few feet behind the window, as if one tiny movement from either of them might reveal their location to the stalker below.

"This is crazy," whispered Cruz. "He can't see us all the way up here."

"You never know." Emmett went up on tiptoe. "I'll see if he's still there." He swayed forward. Cruz grabbed the back of his shirt to steady him. "A little more … a little more … a little more …"

"Emmett!" Cruz gritted his teeth. "Just one more 'a little more' and we'll both be on the floor."

"Reel me in. He's gone."

Once vertical, they rushed to the window. Cruz looked up and down both sides of the street. The man had left.

"Just to be on the safe side." Emmett reached across Cruz to pull the cord to the blinds. As the bamboo shade quickly unfurled, it bumped a few items Cruz had set on the windowsill next to his bed, including the blue box with his mother's things. The box fell, spilling its contents. "Sorry," said Emmett as they dropped to their knees. They quickly gathered up all the items—the cat sticky notes, bandages, almonds, key, crown charm, metal washers.

Emmett picked up the photograph of Cruz and his mother. "Is this you?"

"Yeah, with my mom." Cruz wished he could tell Emmett more about that day, but he didn't remember it.

Emmett snorted. "Nice grape juice mustache."

"Yeah, yeah." Cruz held out his hand for the picture.

"What's on the back?" Emmett had flipped the photograph and was studying it.

"The back?"

"By the looks of these symbols, I'd say it's a—"

"A cipher!" said Cruz. How had he missed it? Although the ink was faded, he had no doubt what it was. Someone had carefully written the entire alphabet, numbers zero through nine, and punctuation marks. Above each character was a different swirling symbol. Some of the swirls went clockwise, others counterclockwise. Some had dots. Some didn't.

"I've never seen one like this," said Emmett.

Cruz wrinkled his brow. He had. "It looks familiar," he said, but couldn't recall where he'd seen it.

THE NEXT MORNING, CRUZ REMEMBERED. Professor Benedict was taking roll in journalism class when it hit him.

"Emmett"—Cruz nudged his friend—"I know where I've seen that cipher."

"Where?"

"In a letter my—"

"Cruz, would you like to assist me with the MC photography demo?" Dr. Benedict asked.

"Sure!" Cruz practically ran to the front of the room. He had read about mind-control digital photography in their text and was eager to try it. Cruz placed the flat, curved metal strip with a lens attached to the right side on his head. The headpiece was so light he barely felt it. Cruz snapped the lens down over his right eye. This move, he knew, automatically turned the camera on.

"The headpiece contains miniature computerized electrodes," said Professor Benedict. "They sync the wearer's neural oscillations, or brain waves, with the *globus pallidus* of the lenticular nucleus. This area of the brain controls the muscles that allow you to blink. Cruz?" She stepped out of the way to let him take it from there.

"To take a photograph," said Cruz, "you point the lens at your subject, think of the word 'photo,' and shut your eyes." Cruz looked at Bryndis sitting in the front row, imagined the word "photo" in his mind, then blinked. Moments later, a blurry photo of Bryndis appeared on the big television screen.

The explorers giggled.

"Oops," said Cruz. "You have to keep your eyes closed for a full two seconds. You can also zoom in and out or lighten or darken the picture by thinking of what you want to do. The headpiece reads your thoughts and obeys."

"Thank you, Cruz," said Professor Benedict. "Good job. You can take that camera and head back to your seat. All right, class, now it's your turn. Please find a partner." As their instructor handed out camera equipment, she explained that they were free to roam the campus and practice their mind photography for the remainder of the class, as long as they didn't disturb other classes or bother the staff. "Your photos will be available to view online moments after you take them," she said. "Be sure to master this skill. This afternoon's CAVE assignment will require you to be proficient at MC photography."

Emmett was tugging at Cruz's sleeve. "What about the cipher? Tell me—"

"Not here," said Cruz.

Emmett and Cruz headed out of class. Once in the library, the teams scattered. Cruz motioned for Emmett to follow him. As they went, they took shots of the library, the hall, the lobby, the elevator, and, finally, their dorm room.

Once he'd closed the door behind them, Cruz tipped his lens up. "Turn off your camera."

Emmett complied. "What's going on?"

Cruz slid the blue box out from under his bed and took out the photograph with the cipher on the back. Opening his bottom dresser drawer, he removed a large red plastic envelope. It was where he kept his important papers, such as awards, certificates, letters, and Aunt Marisol's postcards. He popped the snap and lifted out the cream envelope on top. "Before she died, my mother wrote a letter to me," said Cruz. "She told my dad if anything ever happened to her to give the letter to me on my thirteenth birthday. Since my birthday is November twenty-ninth and my dad knew we'd be on *Orion,* he decided to give the letter to me before I came to the Academy." Cruz opened the flap and removed the parchment.

"What does it say?" gulped Emmett.

"It's what it *doesn't* say," said Cruz, unfolding the page. He laid the photo cipher-side up on his bed, then carefully placed the birthday letter from his mother beside it. "See for yourself."

As Emmett looked from the swirling symbols that bordered the letter to those on the back of the photograph, then back to the letter, his eyes grew. "This is unbelievable! Your mom wrote a coded message to you. I wonder how she knew you'd get it."

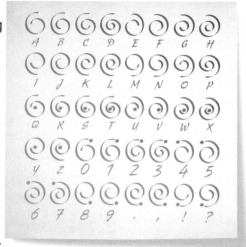

"She must have thought my dad or Aunt Marisol would get her personal belongings from her desk, and once I opened the letter, they'd tell me about the cipher," said Cruz. "She probably didn't figure on Aunt Marisol never opening the box or my dad never reading the letter."

"You mean, you're the only one who knows about the cipher and message?" When Cruz nodded, Emmett let out a whistle.

Cruz grabbed a small spiral notepad and pencil from his desk and hurried back to sit on his bed.

Emmett started to back away. "This is private stuff. I should let you—"

"Oh no you don't. You're in too deep now," said Cruz with a grin. "Besides, this cipher looks tricky."

Emmett flopped beside him.

Cruz was glad he'd asked for Emmett's help. Deciphering the message was painstaking work. Because many of the symbols were similar, it took time to match the swirls from Cruz's birthday letter to the correct ones on the cipher. Just when they thought they'd hit on a match, one of them would realize the swirl ended a fraction of an inch too high or was facing the wrong way or was missing a dot.

"That's an *e*," said Cruz.

"Are you sure? It looks like a *j* to me," said Emmett.

"The *j* swirl goes counterclockwise. See?"

"Yep, you're right." Emmett took off his glasses. "Looking at all these swirls is starting to make my eyes go haywire."

"Do you want to take a break? I can keep working—"

"No." Emmett put his glasses back on.

Finally, after more than an hour of poring over the cipher, they decoded the final symbol. Straightening, Cruz read the message.

> *You are the only one I can entrust with this difficult mission. You are the only one I am certain can endure to the end. Find my journal. Find my life.*
> *Love, Mom*
> *pasc 823912 cslew*

"A journal!" cried Emmett. "Your mom kept a journal. I bet it explains what she was working on that put her in so much danger."

"I hope so," said Cruz. "Do you think she would have given it to Aunt Marisol or my dad?"

"If she had, why didn't she say so in the message?"

Emmett was right. The message directed Cruz to *find* the journal, as if it was buried treasure. *That's it, isn't it?* His mother had tucked her journal away in a secret place for him to uncover. *But where?*

"I wonder what this means," said Emmett, pointing to the last line of the message.

"I know PASC," said Cruz. "Those are my mom's initials. Petra Alexandria Sebastian Coronado. I don't know what the numbers and other letters mean."

Cruz had no idea where to begin looking for the journal. Still, he would not let himself get discouraged. He knew from Aunt Marisol's puzzle postcards that something that completely baffled you one day could become totally clear the next.

Find my journal. Find my life.

"I will, Mom," Cruz said softly.

It was more than a goal. It was a promise.

13

"A HIDDEN

journal?" Sailor froze, a bite of cashew chicken salad inches from her mouth. They were eating lunch in the packed dining hall. "This keeps getting weirder and weirder."

"Tell me about it." Cruz lifted the bun from his cheeseburger to scrape off the dill pickle slices.

"If you're not going to eat those …?" asked Emmett before the trio of crinkle-cut pickles had even hit Cruz's plate.

"They're yours." Cruz pushed his plate toward Emmett, but his roommate was sliding out of his chair.

"Be right back," said Emmett. "I want to get another chili dog before they run out. Gotta get fueled up for today's big mission."

When Emmett was gone, Sailor turned to Cruz. "So how are you going to get in?"

"In?"

"You know …"

Cruz shook his head. He didn't know what she meant.

"The Synthesis," whispered Sailor. "Where else would your mother's journal be?"

Cruz had never considered the Synthesis as a hiding spot for his mom's journal. The place was a fortress. His mom wouldn't have expected him to look for it there, would she? Oh, sure, he'd gotten in once. By accident. Literally. If Sailor's hunch was correct, how was he

supposed to gain access again? It's not like he could go up to the door and knock. Could he?

Less than an hour later, Cruz was outside the CAVE with Emmett and Sailor. This time, it was Dugan who was late. Cruz zipped up his heavy coat. He checked his pockets to be sure he had everything: knit cap, wool scarf, and gloves. Their instructions had told them to prepare for damp and windy conditions, with temperatures below freezing. Cruz had put on three layers of clothing and two pairs of socks. He hoped it was enough.

"Below freezing?" Sailor was reading the prep directions again. "Why can't we go someplace warm? Like Hawaii," she teased, nudging Cruz. "Tell them we want to go where there's warm sand and surf. I bet Kauai is paradise."

"It is," he said matter-of-factly. "And it isn't."

He could tell by her scrunched lips Sailor didn't understand. How could she? Her family was intact. Even someplace as beautiful as Kauai couldn't make up for losing your mother.

"Professor Benedict said this was a new program and we're the first team to try it," said Emmett.

"Let's set the bar high for the rest of the teams," added Sailor, and they all agreed.

They heard clomping. Dugan emerged from the shadows wearing a puffy mint green jacket. A green knit cap with a floppy tassel was pulled down over his ears. Dugan was 12 minutes late. No one said anything, about his outfit or his tardiness, and he offered no apology. With everyone on Team Cousteau present, Renshaw put his Open Sesame band up to the camera. The moment the doors parted, they were blasted by a bitterly cold wind. Putting up a forearm to shield his face, Cruz caught a whiff of salt. He heard seagulls cry. Stepping into the simulator, he felt the sway of wood under his feet. A pier! As the wind subsided, Cruz dropped his arm. To his left, he saw the white-tipped waves of a restless ocean; to the right, a small fishing village.

In front of him towered a sleek, gleaming passenger ship. Cruz did not need to read the name on the bow.

"*Orion,*" he said softly.

A gold stripe ran the length of the vessel, separating the lower section of the navy blue hull from three sparkling white decks and the captain's bridge. On the mast above the bridge, a blue flag with the Academy's gold logo billowed against the vanilla sky.

For a moment, nobody said a word.

Renshaw finally broke the silence. "It's got to be at least a hundred meters long."

"One hundred and eleven, or three hundred sixty-four feet, to be exact," corrected Professor Benedict. She had appeared beside Bryndis in holographic form. "Welcome to Nome, Alaska, in December! You are currently one hundred forty miles from the Arctic Circle and one hundred sixty miles east of Russia. The temperature is nineteen degrees Fahrenheit with winds at twenty knots, so I hope you're all wearing heavy coats."

"We've only been here for two minutes and already I can't feel my toes," Sailor muttered to Cruz.

"Did you say 'toes' or 'nose'?"

"Take your pick. Can we get on the boat already?"

"If you haven't figured it out, today's exercise will take you aboard the Academy's flagship expedition vessel," said Professor Benedict. "You're now in your third week of training, and you'll be boarding the real thing in a little over a week, so what better way to get accustomed to shipboard life than here in the simulator?"

Cruz applauded. He couldn't wait to get on the ship for real and begin traveling the world! Everyone else on Team Cousteau was clapping, too—except Emmett. He was trying to wipe the frost off his glasses.

"Your mission today will be twofold," said Professor Benedict. "First, follow the glowing yellow arrows and take a complete tour of the ship. Soon it will be your home away from home, so get to know it. Visit everything from the observation deck to the explorers' cabins to the CAVE."

Dugan's jaw dropped. "There's a CAVE on *Orion*?"

"Yes, although it's far smaller than this one. We use it for training and recreation between ports of call," explained their instructor. "Your second task is more challenging. You are to imagine you are a freelance journalist and photographer for a conservation magazine. Your assignment is to find a news story aboard *Orion*."

"What kind of story?" asked Renshaw.

"That, Mr. McKittrick, is up to you," she said, the corners of her lips sliding up. "A good journalist is always on the lookout for a juicy and important issue to report on. There are many interesting holo-passengers and crew aboard the ship. Talk to them. Perhaps one will spark an idea. Or you may choose to focus on a feature of the ship—for instance, *Ridley*, the deep-water submersible craft." She paced the dock. "Remember, the magazine for which you are writing is dedicated to conservation. You must also take photographs with the mind control cameras to complement your story. You'll find the photography equipment available to check out at the purser's desk. After the mission, you will write a five-hundred-word article and process three photographs to go along with it. The assignment must be submitted by tomorrow morning at nine a.m. Any questions?"

"Can we work in teams?" asked Bryndis.

"No," said their teacher. "This is an individual project. You may take the tour together, but after that you are to split up to do your stories. Please do not collaborate or intentionally select the same topic as another teammate. Any other questions?"

When no one spoke, Professor Benedict's image began to dissolve. "Bon voyage, explorers!"

"I hope they have hot chocolate on the ship," said Sailor, bouncing on her toes to keep warm.

"It would technically be virtual cocoa," said Emmett, which earned him a dirty look from Sailor.

"I've got dibs on Ridley for my news story," said Dugan.

Renshaw put up a hand. "Dibs on the captain for mine."

"I'll take the research labs," said Bryndis. "If that's okay with everyone else."

"I think I'd like the observation deck," chimed in Sailor.

"Good choice," Renshaw said to her. "You'll probably see a lot when we go through the Bering Strait."

"Where are you going?" Emmett asked Cruz.

"I don't know yet," said Cruz. He didn't want to pick anything easy or obvious. Professor Benedict had suggested they talk to some of the passengers, so she must have had good reason for it.

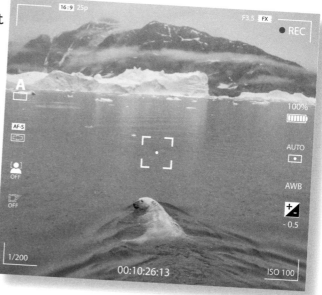

Boarding the ship, Cruz and Emmett stuck together for the self-guided tour. They followed the arrows down to the lowest deck, B deck, to see the engine room and submersible, then began working their way back up. Above B deck was the main deck, home to the mini CAVE, housekeeping and laundry, the crew's quarters, and the lounge. After that, it was another flight up to the second deck. Taking a right off the sunny, open atrium, the pair headed down the stern passage to get a look at the explorers' cabins.

"Pretty cushy, huh?" said Emmett, bouncing on one of the two beds in a maple-paneled stateroom. "I hope we get to stay roommates."

Outside on the veranda, leaning on the brass rail, Cruz was about to agree when a bellowing horn startled him. He felt the ship tremble. Foam was churning up from the bottom of the boat. They were under way!

Cruz stayed at the rail, watching the fishing village grow smaller. The ship plowed through rough, steel gray waves, following the rocky, wind-battered coast. Every now and then, the bow hit a small chunk of ice, easily breaking it apart. Beyond the shore, low snow-covered hills stretched miles into the horizon. The stark white landscape was a world away from anything Cruz had ever seen. As the ship continued on its journey, his heart began to pound in anticipation of what was around the next bend. Suddenly, Cruz saw a white blob surface in the waves off the starboard bow. *Is that a . . . ?*

"Emmett!" called Cruz. "There's a polar bear out here! Come here. You gotta see this!"

Cruz snapped a bunch of photos of the polar bear swimming toward shore. A few minutes later, when Emmett still hadn't joined him, Cruz stepped back into the cabin. "Hey, Emmett, you're missing the—"

His roommate was backed into a corner behind the door, his face pinched and his glasses a dull sand color. Emmett gripped his tablet so tightly Cruz was certain the screen was going to crack. "What's wrong?" he asked.

"I didn't know we were going to . . . nobody said anything about leaving port."

"Uh . . . Professor Benedict *did* say we were going on a journey and she *did* say bon voyage, which means—"

"I know what it means."

"Do you want to go to the sick bay? I think it's two decks up. I can check . . ." Cruz dived for his tablet. They still had three decks to go on their tour.

"I'm okay." Emmett's forehead sparkled with sweat.

"Maybe we should get you out of the CAVE," said Cruz, although he had no idea how to do such a thing. The simulator was like a roller coaster. It didn't exactly stop for you to get off.

"I'll be fine," said Emmett. "We'd better go find our stories. You go ahead. I'll be out in a . . . in a . . ." His stomach gurgled.

"Emmett?"

Cheeks bulging, Emmett slapped a hand to his mouth. Staggering past Cruz into the bathroom, he threw up. It was, by upchucking standards, impressive. Emmett hurled pretty much everything he'd had for lunch, which was, by Cruz's count, three chili dogs, a serving of curly fries, a slice of strawberry cheesecake, 16 ounces of grape soda, and Cruz's three pickles.

Shuffling out of the bathroom, Emmett eased himself onto the bed he'd bounced on minutes before. "Sorry."

"It's okay with me, though I'm not sure the Academy's going to be thrilled about what just went down in their virtual bathroom."

"Not a problem." Emmett laid his head on the pillow. "I've seen the CAVE schematics. The toilets are always connected to real 3-D pipes."

That's a relief.

Cruz unfolded a velvet navy throw that had been draped across the corner of a chair. He put it over Emmett, then took a seat in one of the two overstuffed navy chairs in the little seating area. Cruz knew Emmett needed rest, but he was starting to grow concerned about time. They needed to get going on their articles soon.

"I know what you're thinking," Emmett said weakly. "Why does a guy who gets seasick the second we weigh anchor apply to a program where he'll have to spend months at sea?"

Cruz made a face. "Well..."

"I guess you could say I've been obsessed with coming to the Academy since I was five years old," he said. "I know everything about it: its founding and history, the name of every professor who ever taught here, even how tall the main building is—eighty-seven feet including the top spire. Being here is all I've ever wanted. My parents, though... they don't think I can do it."

"I'm sure that's not true—"

"Oh, they know I'm smart enough. But they don't think I'm strong enough to handle the physical part. Maybe they're right."

"No." Cruz was firm. "They're not."

Emmett threw a hand over his eyes. "I had it all worked out. I've got a seasick band for when we board the ship for real, but I didn't bring it today. If I'd known we were coming on *Orion*—" His voice broke.

"Relax, Emmett. It could happen to any of us," said Cruz. "I'm sure they'll understand."

"Motion sickness was one of the things they asked about on the application. I didn't want to take the chance they'd reject me, so I . . . I lied. I can't tell the truth. Not now. What if they send me home?"

"Okay. Let's think for a minute." Cruz rubbed his chin. "We just have to get you through this mission."

Emmett had his hand over his mouth again. "Good luck."

Setting his elbows on his knees, Cruz clasped his hands and rested his face against his wrist. The OS band felt cool against his cheek. There must be *something* they could do. *Wait a minute . . .*

"Emmett, did you say a seasick *band*?"

"Uh-huh."

Cruz turned his arm over. "So you wear it on your wrist?"

"Yeah. It sends electrical impulses through the median nerve to the brain. The pulses interfere with the nauseous signals coming from the stomach to the brain to keep you from feeling sick." Emmett slowly lowered his hand. He stared at his own gold bracelet. He was beginning to understand.

"Taryn said the OS band does everything from count calories to monitor *brain function*," said Cruz. "Couldn't you hack into it and rig it to do the same thing the seasick band does?"

"Possibly. Maybe. I don't know. It's a long shot—"

"Right now, it's our only shot to get you back on your feet."

"I could give it a try."

Cruz knew one of Emmett's "tries" was worth 10,000 of his own best efforts. He handed him his tablet. Emmett glanced up. "Cruz, could you get me another pillow so I can sit up?"

Cruz grabbed the pillow from the other bed.

"And my water? I left my stuff downstairs."

"I'm on it," said Cruz.

They had both left their packs at the purser's desk near the lounge one deck down. Checking to make sure the coast was clear, Cruz stepped into the passage. He hurried along the narrow corridor, quickly glancing into each of the cabins. He saw no one else from Team Cousteau. Taking the sharp turn at the end of the passage, Cruz ran smack into a member of the crew. "I'm sorry, I didn't mean to—" Cruz gasped.

The scarred man!

Cruz rubbed his ribs. "Are . . . are you virtual or r-real?"

"I can assure you I am very, very real."

14

"WE'RE ON v-video, you know," sputtered Cruz.

"Not here, we aren't."

"How do you know?"

"Let's just say I am familiar with this particular program. We don't have much time. I thought I made it clear you needed to leave the Academy."

"Sorry ... but I'm not going to do that. I can't ... What difference does it make to you what I do anyway?"

"I care about what happens to you." His gruff manner softened. "I worried about your mother, too. We were colleagues and friends. Cruz, I'm Elistair Fallowfeld."

"Fallowfeld?" Cruz shook his head. "You're lying. Dr. Fallowfeld is dead."

"No, he—I—am very much alive." He put a hand to the rough craters on his neck. "I was injured in the lab accident that killed your mother, but I recovered."

"But they told us you'd—"

"It was to protect me."

"What *were* you and my mother working on?"

"Nothing. I mean, I don't know what *she* was working on. We weren't collaborating. I helped her with a problem now and then. Bits and

129

pieces, that's all I ever got—never the full picture. Her lab was restricted to top-level personnel, her work locked away every night."

Locked away? Maybe Sailor *was* right and his mom's journal was still there.

"Dr. Fallowfeld, I have to get into the Synthesis," said Cruz.

"The Synthesis? Why?"

Cruz still wasn't sure he could trust this man. "I . . . I need to see where my mom worked."

"I'm afraid that's impossible. Her lab and office—that whole section of the Synthesis—was destroyed in the fire."

Cruz felt as if he'd been punched in the jaw. Fire. That was how she had died. That's why Dr. Fallowfeld's hands and neck were disfigured.

"I can see you didn't know," said Dr. Fallowfeld. "I'm sorry, Cruz. Truly, I am. I was there when it happened. I was in—"

"Don't say it. Don't say you were in the wrong place at the wrong time."

"I was going to say I was in the lab next to hers. I tried to save her, but the security doors were jammed and it was bulletproof glass . . ."

Cruz backed away. Part of him wanted to know the details. Another part of him wanted to run as far as he could as fast as he could.

"By the time I got to her ..." He shook his head. "The last thing she said to me was, 'Nebula is behind this. You must protect Cruz. They'll go after him when they realize ...'"

"Realize what?" prompted Cruz.

"I don't know. After your mom's death, your dad said he was taking you to Hawaii. I figured that was far enough away from whatever your mom was concerned about. When I found out you were a student at the Academy, I knew I had to warn you about Nebula. Have they tried anything?"

"Yes. Someone *is* after me," said Cruz. "Who is Nebula anyway?"

"Not who. What. Nebula is—" He stopped when the lights around them dimmed. The passageway disappeared and they caught a glimpse of black CAVE walls before the ship fully reappeared. "That's odd," said Dr. Fallowfeld. "We'd better go. You've been out of video range for too long. The cameras will be looking for you."

"This mission isn't going well." Cruz sighed. "Emmett is seasick and we have to finish our journalism assignment ..."

Dr. Fallowfeld stepped aside to let him pass. "You want the story

of the century? Find Dr. Louis Osment. Thick beard. Red cap. He's the world's leading expert on climate change." He read Cruz's quizzical look. "I wrote this software program."

"So then ... you could calm the ocean for Emmett?"

"I could." For the first time since Cruz had met him, he grinned. "All right. I will."

Cruz began climbing the stairs. Halfway up, he stopped. "Hey! You never told me about Nebula." He peered over the rail. "Dr. Fallowfeld?"

Dr. Elistair Fallowfeld was gone.

WRAPPED IN THE comfort of a plush olive green wingback the next day, Cruz closed his eyes. The chair had become his favorite thinking spot, a quiet place of refuge when the dorm wing got too noisy. It was tucked in an alcove in the fantasy section of the library. Cruz had stumbled upon it once when he'd taken a wrong turn in the computer technology section. He'd gotten lost in the labyrinth of shelves. The tufted green chair looked new, making Cruz suspect he was the first explorer to find it.

Cruz knew he should be on his way to journalism. The break between classes was almost over. He couldn't seem to gather the energy to face what was coming.

"Cruz!" Mr. Rook nearly dropped an armload of books. "I'm not used to seeing anyone back here."

Cruz ran his hand along the armrest. "Good chair."

"Picked it out myself a few years back. I'm surprised more explorers don't use it, but then there is a bit of a maze to get through to discover it, isn't there?" The librarian began reshelving books. "Don't you have afternoon classes in a few minutes?"

"Yeah." Cruz tipped his head back and forth to indicate he wasn't all that motivated to go.

"Ah, I see." Mr. Rook slid a book into place. "You know, most of the faculty here are former explorers with degrees from Harvard or Oxford. Not me. I never attended the Academy. I don't have a doctorate. I went to community college and got my undergraduate and master's degrees from the University of Hawaii."

Cruz sat up. "*I'm* from Hawaii."

"Really? That is a coincidence, isn't it?" His books put away, Mr. Rook leaned against the bookcase. He folded his arms. "Want to talk about it? You know, with an average, ordinary guy from home?"

Cruz didn't know where to begin. The CAVE mission had not gone well, and it had nothing to do with running into the elusive Dr. Fallowfeld. The good news: Emmett *was* able to hack into his OS band and get it to send electrical pulses to his brain. The bad news: Instead of curing his seasickness, it had caused some kind of an allergic reaction. Within minutes, Emmett's whole body was covered in red hives. Fortunately, Dr. Fallowfeld had kept his word and calmed the virtual seas, so Emmett did start to feel better, except for the itching part. Knowing they were short on time, Cruz had let his roommate have the climate change story with Dr. Osment, and he did his article about the ship's reinforced hull. Aunt Marisol had once told him that *Orion* was an ice-class ship, meaning it could break through even the thickest sea ice and take scientists to the most remote parts of the world. It was a decent topic, but Cruz hadn't had enough time to do the story justice. He'd helped a still shaky, über-itchy Emmett find Dr. Osment and get photos, which left Cruz less than 10 minutes to do his own story. He rushed through his interview with the first mate and barely made it to the front of the ship to snap a few photos of the bow before their time was up.

Cruz looked at Mr. Rook. "Our teachers have us review our CAVE videos in class," he told him. "If I go to journalism today, everyone is going to get to watch a disaster movie starring me. It'll be the second one. Talk about simulation humiliation."

"You didn't die again, did you?"

Cruz winced. "You heard about that mission?"

Mr. Rook chuckled, as if to say news traveled fast in a small school. "I wouldn't be so hard on yourself. The training is tough."

"It is, but it's fun, too."

"So it must be your teacher who's giving you a rough time?"

"Professor Benedict? No, she's great. She'll ask questions and challenge you to think about things from a different viewpoint. We've had some good discussions about fair and accurate reporting and ethics."

"Sounds interesting."

"It is! Last week, we talked about whether it was right to alter a photo, even if you are touching up things that won't affect the story, like fixing the background or erasing someone who is photobombing—" Cruz stopped. "I know what you're doing. You're getting me to point out all the positive things about class so I can see they outweigh the negative ones."

"Pretty obvious, huh?" The librarian glanced at his watch and clicked his tongue. "It's almost two."

"All right, I'm going." Cruz pushed himself out of the chair. "I guess I can endure one more simulation humiliation."

"Thatta way."

"By the way, for the record, this time I did not die."

"See? Another positive. I'll keep the chair warm for you," he called after Cruz.

Cruz had nothing to fear regarding public embarrassment. Professor Benedict didn't play any of the explorers' videos from their last CAVE mission. *Whew!* However, as class wound down, she did say,

"Your articles are now graded and available online."

On his tablet, Cruz found his name on the class list, clicked on it, and put in his password: *Lani*. His article came up. Professor Benedict's notes at the top came as no surprise:

> *Your writing is strong, Cruz, but your reporting needs to be more in-depth. There were several biologists, botanists, and climatologists aboard who could have added dimension to your story. Don't be afraid to interview them. On the plus side, your photos are spectacular! The polar bear shots look like a professional took them. Well done!*
>
> > *Grade: B+*
> >
> > *—KB*

Cruz promised himself that he would do better next time. Besides, the B plus was worth helping Emmett get through his crisis. Cruz closed the file and turned to Emmett, who was all smiles.

"She liked my angle on the warming of the Bering Sea and the food chain," said his roommate. "Dr. Osment said this year is the warmest on record for the Bering Sea, meaning a decrease in zooplankton for fish to eat, which means less fish for birds, seals, and other wildlife to eat. He said the sea ice is melting so fast that if things don't turn around, polar bears could go extinct in our lifetime."

"Extinct?" Cruz was dumbstruck. "I can't imagine not having polar bears on Earth."

"Scary stuff, huh?"

Professor Benedict's head appeared between them. "I'd like to see both of you after class," she said softly.

Emmett and Cruz exchanged fearful looks. Cruz had a feeling they were going to get in trouble for not getting Emmett to the sick bay during their last CAVE mission. What else could it be? Cruz racked his brain for other possibilities but couldn't think of any. When class ended, he looked down at his tablet to discover he hadn't taken any notes. Maybe this time Renshaw would let *him* borrow *his* notes.

Once everyone in the class had emptied out, Dr. Benedict took the chair next to Emmett. "I understand you were ... uh, unwell ... during the CAVE mission."

Emmett's head dropped. "Uh-huh."

"And, Cruz, you were with him at the time it occurred?"

"Yes."

"Why didn't you use the CAVE emergency protocol?" she asked.

Cruz bit his lip. "There's a CAVE emergency protocol?"

"You squeeze the sides of your OS band's screen and say 'CAVE emergency,'" said their professor.

"How could I have forgotten about that? It was in the orientation video," added Emmett.

"Oh." Between being followed by Nebula, running into Dr. Fallowfeld, learning his mom had kept a journal, and doing his schoolwork, Cruz had forgotten to watch the video.

"It's my fault," Emmett piped up. "Cruz wanted to go for help, but I said no. I didn't want anyone to know I was seasick."

"I get that," said Dr. Benedict. "I've gotten a little woozy on *Orion* myself a few times, for real. But the last thing you want to do while we are traveling is hide a health issue. I can speak for the whole faculty in telling you that it won't affect your grade. If you or a fellow explorer ever has a health problem, even one you might think is minor, you are to get medical attention as soon as possible, okay?"

Emmett and Cruz vowed they would.

On their way out of the library, Emmett turned to Cruz. "Do you think I'll get in trouble with Taryn?"

"Nah," said Cruz, though he wasn't totally sure. "From here on out, take your seasick band to all CAVE missions."

Emmett crossed his heart.

AFTER DINNER, WHILE EMMETT AND CRUZ were studying for the next day's biology quiz on biomes, Taryn appeared at their open door. Cruz figured she'd come to talk to Emmett about his motion sickness. Should he leave them alone?

"Dr. Hightower wants to see you," said Taryn.

A look of fear crossing his face, Emmett slowly rose.

"Not you," said Taryn. She pointed to Cruz. "You."

"Me?" Cruz choked. "Why?"

Taryn lifted a shoulder.

"This is because of me, isn't it?" Emmett reached for his jacket. "I'd better come with you."

"No." Taryn was stern. "She only requested Cruz."

Dr. Hightower's office was on the top floor of the administration building. Okay, it *was* the top floor. When the elevator doors parted, Cruz stepped into a massive black marble foyer. There was no one at the tall pedestal of a reception desk; however, the double doors behind it were open.

"Come in, Cruz," boomed Dr. Hightower's voice.

Inching toward the doors, his eyes tracked up to read the motto in gold above them: EXPLORER ACADEMY. TO DISCOVER. TO INNOVATE. TO PROTECT.

Cruz stepped into an oval room almost the size of their dining hall. It smelled like lavender. The curved walls were made of black marble and almost every space was covered with something: framed certificates, awards, photographs, or bookshelves. In the middle of the room was an arched flagstone fireplace. There was no fire burning inside.

Underfoot, a gray cement floor had been polished to a high shine. The only real color in the room came from a glass chandelier at least 10 feet high and twice as wide. Thousands of crystals seemed to be crying blue and green tears onto a square of eight cushioned gray chairs below. At the far end of the oval, Dr. Hightower stood behind a curved black mahogany desk wearing her signature cream jacket and matching turtleneck.

"Have a seat."

Crossing the mammoth room, Cruz chose a rigid, steel gray chair next to a huge freestanding globe. Earth was tipped on its axis in a cherry wood base, the continents of the world glowing sapphire blue against golden seas. He longed to reach out and spin the enormous planet, but he didn't. Cruz was nervous. His mind was racing. His palms were sweaty.

Dr. Hightower sat tall in her black leather throne of a chair and switched on a small lamp next to her—a group of blue metal herons in flight. "Cruz, I received some rather disappointing news today—"

"He was seasick and covered in hives!" burst Cruz. "I was only trying to get him through the mission, that's all. The Academy motto says explorers are supposed to protect, and that's what I was doing: trying to protect my friend." He knew he was talking too fast and too loudly, but he couldn't stop. He couldn't bear for her to be angry with him. "I'm sorry I didn't call for help, Dr. Hightower, but I forgot to watch the orientation video and I know I should have because then I would have known the proper protocol but I know what to do now, and like I told Dr. Benedict, it won't happen again. I promise."

There. He had said it. Cruz felt so much better now that everything was out in the open.

Dr. Hightower was looking at him strangely. "What are you talking about?"

"You know, helping Emmett when he got sick in the CAVE."

Her mouth was turned down.

Cruz matched her frown with his own. "Isn't that why I'm here?"

"No." She clasped her hands. "You're here because someone hacked into the CAVE software and tampered with the programs for Team Cousteau's training missions."

"Really?" Cruz gasped. "That's awful."

"Professor Gabriel noticed an issue in one of your mission videos, and when it happened again in Professor Benedict's training, we decided to take a closer look."

"Issue? Was it like a . . . a flicker?"

"That was part of it."

"I saw them. We all did. There was a glitch in the program when we were on the butterfly mission and then again on *Orion*."

"Our investigation discovered the hacker altered these exercises to make them easier for Team Cousteau," she explained. "I'm sure I don't need to tell you that at the Academy, we take something like this very seriously."

"Of course." Cruz shifted. He didn't like the way she was looking at him. "So . . . you want to know if I know anything about it?"

"Actually, Cruz, I know everything I need to."

"Oh." He didn't get it. *Then why am I here?*

"Our experts traced the hack to your tablet."

"M-my tablet? But—"

"It's over. We have the proof. We *know* you're the one responsible."

"But . . . I . . . I didn't do it . . . I would never—"

Dr. Hightower held up her hand. "Denials will get you nowhere, explorer." She set her jaw. "Cruz Coronado, it deeply saddens me to inform you that you have been expelled from the Academy."

15

CRUZ was numb.

Dr. Hightower continued speaking, calmly and with the perfect amount of disapproving parent in her tone. Everything had been arranged. His father and Aunt Marisol had been informed of the situation. Cruz was to go back to his dorm and pack his things. Aunt Marisol would pick him up in one hour. His father would fly in to take him home.

"My dad? Is coming here?"

"Next weekend, I believe," Dr. Hightower said. "You'll stay with your aunt until he arrives. Do you have anything you would like to say to me?"

Cruz was in shock. It felt like he was on an out-of-control carousel. Everything was a blur of lights and shapes and colors. He couldn't think and he couldn't get off. Minutes ago, Cruz was an elite explorer, one of the next generation of trailblazers destined to change the world. Now he wasn't. "I... I didn't do it, Dr. Hightower," he sputtered. "I'm telling you, I didn't hack into the CAVE—"

"Have you forgotten it already, Cruz?"

"Forgotten?"

"Our cornerstone: above all, honor." Her eyes searched his. "There is honor in truth, you know, even if it cannot alter the consequences."

"I *am* telling the truth. There must be some mistake."

"We do not make mistakes," she clipped. "The evidence is incontrovertible. The board has thoroughly reviewed it in detail and has made its ruling. As I explained to your father, you may appeal, of course, but..." She shook her head, implying he would likely lose if he did. Dr. Hightower ran a hand through her stiff white hair. "I had hoped you would be forthcoming with me. It wouldn't have changed the outcome, of course, but it would have shown strength of character to admit what you had done."

"But I *didn't*—"

"So you've said." Her icy tone sent a chill through him. "If you have nothing to confess—I mean, say—you may go. You'll need to get packed."

Cruz stood slowly, unsure if his legs would hold him. Somehow, they did. Somehow, they took him across the vast office, under the crying crystal chandelier and past all the awards and certificates and the fireplace with no fire. His mind was spinning. Who could have done this? And why? Dr. Fallowfeld was the most obvious suspect. He had two strikes. First, he'd admitted he had a hand in designing some of the CAVE software, and second, he had motive: He wanted Cruz to go home. Maybe he figured if he couldn't convince Cruz to leave on his own, then he would force him out. Yet Dr. Fallowfeld didn't seem like the kind of person who could be that mean. Of course, Nebula had proved it certainly *could* be that mean...

If Cruz could get the Academy president to see he had enemies, maybe she would give him time to uncover the truth. Cruz whirled around. "Dr. Hightower—"

"Good *night,* Mr. Coronado." She swiveled her chair to face the wall behind her.

Cruz stared at the back of the black throne. He had been officially dismissed by Regina M. Hightower, Ph.D., the president of Explorer Academy. Not yet out the door and he had already been erased from school history. The judgment was final. Cruz knew he would find no mercy here.

When he got back to the room, Emmett was not there. Cruz got his suitcase down from the top shelf in his closet, flung it onto his bed, and

began throwing in clothes. He was angry and confused and very, very hurt. How could this have happened? Who was behind it? And why? Maybe Aunt Marisol could help him make sense of it all...

"Hey, will you try my lolly cake?" Sailor stood at the door holding a plate of what looked like sliced brown cookies with bits of colored marshmallows inside. "I've been trying to tell everyone it doesn't have lollipops in it, but...What's going on?"

Cruz yanked open the top drawer of his dresser. "I'm being kicked out of school."

"*What?*" The cookies nearly slid to the floor. Righting the plate, Sailor dumped it onto his desk. "What happened?"

Scooping up his socks, he dropped them into his suitcase. "Somebody hacked into the CAVE software and messed with our team's training programs. They traced the hack to my tablet."

"You? That's crazy. It's gotta be a mistake."

"That's what I told Dr. Hightower. She said the Academy never makes mistakes...right before she expelled me. Or was it after? I guess it doesn't matter now that I'm out, does it?"

"Never?" She snorted. "They thought I was a boy, remember? Believe me, they make mistakes, all right. But who would do that? And how?"

"I've been racking my brain. I guess someone could have logged on to my tablet in the library or in my room when I wasn't around. Me? A hacker? That's a laugh. I couldn't even hack into Emmett's OS band when he was sea—*Ahhh!*"

"What?" prompted Sailor.

"I just realized...I couldn't hack into Emmett's OS band, but he could. And did. And if Emmett can hack into that, then..." Cruz began to pace. "It all makes sense."

Sailor's face was squished in. "Not to me, it doesn't. What are you talking about?"

"In the CAVE, on *Orion*, when Emmett got sick, I said the Academy wasn't going to be thrilled that he spewed in their simulator, and he said the toilets were always piped because he had *seen the schematics*. He knows that system backward and forward."

"Yeah, but that doesn't mean—"

"And who has access to your stuff more than your own roommate?" Cruz clapped his hands. "I wonder how long he's been planning this. Was it since that first day that we met at the airport? I'll bet. I'll bet he's been just sneaking around—"

"Wait!" Sailor shook her head. "Do you hear yourself?"

Cruz was too busy talking to hear anything. "He said something to me about perfectionists once—that they were never satisfied with being good. They had to be great. He joked that he used to be one. Maybe he still is. Maybe he had to be sure he was great."

"You're upset. That's why you're making all these wild accusations, but I'm telling you Emmett wouldn't do that to you," insisted Sailor. "You're overreacting. Someone else has to be behind this."

"Like who?"

"I don't know . . . it could be anyone in your wing . . . Ali, Zane, Dugan . . ." She pointed at Cruz. "Yes, what about Dugan? He's got it in for you, especially after you whipped his frosting in the ARC."

"Dugan?" Cruz supposed it was a possibility, but Dugan didn't have anywhere near the tech skills that Emmett had.

Cruz's phone was ringing. It was his father. "Hi, Dad." His voice broke.

"Cruz? Are you all right?"

Hearing the worry in his dad's voice, tears sprang to Cruz's eyes. He fought them back. "I'm okay."

"Your aunt is on her way."

"I didn't do anything wrong, Dad. I didn't cheat."

"You don't have to tell me that." His voice relaxed. "The one thing I know you're not is a cheater. You don't even fudge on your scorecard when we play putt-putt golf. It's not how you're wired. Besides, you live for a good challenge. You've never taken the easy route, even when you could."

It was true. In school, when other kids were peeking in the back of their math textbooks for the answers, Cruz refused. He would work and work until he figured out the problem for himself. He never wanted anyone to do it for him or even give him a hint. Where was the fun in that? That's what made Aunt Marisol's puzzle postcards so great. It might take him a while to crack a cipher—days or even weeks—but eventually he would get it. The tougher the puzzle, the more satisfying it was when you solved it.

"I tried to tell Dr. Hightower that but she wouldn't budge," said his dad. "I did my best to convince her to let you stay, but—"

"You did? You want me...to stay? But I...I thought—"

"I'll admit I was apprehensive about you going back...there...but I knew I couldn't stand in your way. Your mother would never forgive me. Hey, a delivery just rolled up. Can I call you later at your aunt's?"

"Sure."

"It's gonna be all right, son. Don't worry."

"I know." Cruz tried to keep his voice steady.

"I love you."

"Love you, too, Dad." Biting his lip, Cruz hung up.

"Your dad sounds nice," said Sailor wistfully.

"He is." Cruz rubbed his warm forehead. All he'd ever wanted was to make his dad proud of him. This is not how things were supposed to go.

"You survived, thank goodness!" Emmett flew into the room. He glanced at Sailor's plate on Cruz's desk. "Dr. Hightower gave you cookies?"

Cruz went to his dresser, yanked out the third drawer, and started grabbing folded pairs of jeans.

"What's the matter?" asked Emmett.

"He got expelled," said Sailor.

"*What?* No. No, no, *no!* Is this because of me? I'll talk to Dr. Hightower. I'll explain to her how I got sick on the boat and you were only trying to help. I'll go right now—"

"Forget about being seasick." Cruz flung his jeans into his suitcase. "This has nothing to do with that. I got kicked out because...*someone* hacked into the CAVE software and tampered with Team Cousteau's missions, and they used my tablet to do it."

Emmett's jaw dropped. "They did?"

"Yeah. And you can quit pretending you don't know anything about it."

"Pretending? You mean you think I hacked into the software?"

"Who else?" Cruz started rattling off reasons. "You've got the technical knowledge, you've seen the CAVE schematics, you've got twenty-four seven access to my tablet, and . . . and . . . and you're jealous of me because I'm better at sports than you are." He wasn't at all sure about that last one, but Cruz was angry and it sort of popped out.

"That's . . . that's . . . You're crazy!" cried Emmett. "I can't believe you'd even think for a second I'd do something like that. After all the stuff we've been through? We're teammates. We're friends."

Cruz grunted. "I *thought* we were."

"I'm no cheater."

"Says you." Cruz threw a shoe, end over end, at his suitcase. It hit the rim and bounced onto the floor with a clunk.

Emmett stalked toward the door and nearly collided with Taryn, who was coming in. Hubbard was with her, carrying his favorite tennis ball in his mouth. Emmett bent slightly to put a hand on Hubbard's head. Pausing at the door, he glanced back. All the color was draining from his glasses. Emmett's frames looked like two melting ladles connected in the middle. They were clear. Absolutely clear. Cruz had never seen them do that before. As their eyes met, Cruz expected to see anger in Emmett's eyes. Instead, he saw hurt. A second later, Emmett was gone.

Taryn cleared her throat. "Sailor, if I could have a minute with Cruz?"

"Sure," said Sailor. "I'll be outside if you need me." She grabbed her tray of lolly cake and scooted out.

Taryn closed the door. "I'm so very sorry," she said softly.

Exhausted, Cruz collapsed into his desk chair. Hubbard trotted to him and dropped his fuzzy, lime green ball at Cruz's feet. Looking into the pair of sweet dark eyes peering up at him, Cruz's heart burst at the seams. All of the feelings and emotions he'd been holding back began to pour out—frustration, embarrassment, sadness, anger, misery. He couldn't stop them. He couldn't stop the tears.

Taryn was handing him a tissue. He took one. "I didn't hack into the CAVE software," he choked, wiping his eyes.

"I believe you," she said.

Cruz rolled the ball for Hubbard, who eagerly chased it across the room. He was sure going to miss this pup.

"You could appeal, you know," said Taryn, but even *her* voice held barely a twinge of hope. "Sleep on it. Things will look better in the morning."

Cruz doubted it.

His phone chimed. He had a text. "It's my aunt. She's downstairs."

"Guess we'd better get this done, huh? Left wrist, please." Her voice broke.

Cruz held out his arm. Taryn took a metal square from her hip pocket, placed it over his OS band, and pressed it down. He heard a snap and the gold bracelet fell into her hand. Indescribable pain sliced through his chest.

"I'll need your tablet, too."

Cruz went to his desk and got the computer. "Will you do me a favor?"

"Name it."

"It has my holo-video ad on it for anthro. I was going to turn it in to my aunt. I know it doesn't matter anymore, but would you—?"

"I'll make sure she gets it."

Cruz finished packing. Zipping up the sides of his suitcase, Cruz reached for his jacket. He slipped Mell into his pocket and pinned the remote to the lapel. His hand shook so hard he could hardly attach it. Cruz tucked his mother's box under his arm, and then somehow managed to say, "I'm ready."

Taryn opened the door for him.

Cruz heard a whimper. Hubbard had brought his tennis ball back to him. Bending, Cruz scratched the dog between his ears for the last time. "Sorry, buddy, I won't be able to play anymore. I'll sure miss you when I'm…" He couldn't say the word "gone." Tears blurring his vision, Cruz reached for his suitcase. "Bye, Taryn."

"Goodbye. A word to the wise? Don't let anybody tell you who you are or aren't, okay?"

"Okay. Thanks, Taryn. For everything."

She touched his shoulder. "So long, truth seeker."

Naturally, the news of Cruz's expulsion had traveled quickly. As Cruz rolled his suitcase down the hallway, many of the other boys—Zane, Matteo, Ali, Seth, and even Dugan—came out to say goodbye. Emmett, however, had not stuck around.

Sailor was holding the elevator door for Cruz. He stepped inside and she hit the button for the lobby. The door closed. They rode down in silence and stepped out of the elevator. Maybe Sailor was right. Maybe Emmett wasn't the hacker and Cruz was grasping for an answer, because he needed one right now. It felt unreal. Was he really walking through the lobby for the last time? He remembered how excited he'd been to come through those doors, how he'd stood on the hieroglyphic rug waiting to check in, how strange his wrist had felt when Taryn had snapped on the OS band. Cruz touched the spot near his double-helix birthmark where the band had been. His arm felt weird without it. Naked. Cold. The indentation in his skin was already disappearing.

Could this be happening? Could his life as an explorer end before it had ever truly begun?

At the main doors, Sailor gave him a hug. "It sure was sweet as to know you."

"Same here."

Sniffling, she brushed her eyes with the back of her hand. "Stay in touch?"

Cruz said he would, but he didn't know if he could keep that promise. Sailor, Emmett, Bryndis, Zane, Renshaw, Dugan, Matteo, Ali—all of them were going to live his dream. They were going to do everything he wanted to do and be everything he wanted to be.

Pushing the door open, Cruz stepped out into the cool fall air. Aunt Marisol's red hybrid was parked on the street just beyond the steps. She said little as they loaded his things into her trunk, other than that it would be all right and they would talk things over later. He didn't sense she was angry. Aunt Marisol was like his dad. Neither was big on the silent treatment. If they had something to say to you, they said it. He got into the front seat of the vehicle.

As his aunt pulled away from the curb, Cruz took one last look back at the Academy. His eyes traveled up the steps and grand columns to the fifth floor, to the last window on the left. The shade was down in the Mount Everest room, the light still on. He thought he saw a figure move past the window but couldn't be sure. Cruz was going to miss Emmett Lu, with his wild glasses and endless stomach and silly socks. If Emmett *was* the hacker, it was a crushing betrayal. And if he wasn't . . .

Well, if he wasn't, Cruz had just lost the closest thing to a brother he'd ever had.

16

"THEY CAN'T do that!" Even on his phone screen he could see Lani's nostrils flare. "You have rights, you know."

"Take it easy. I'm not going to jail." A shiver went through him. Was he? Dr. Hightower hadn't said anything about arresting him, but wasn't hacking a crime? Maybe getting expelled from the Academy was only the beginning . . .

"So what's the plan?" asked Lani.

Tapping the speakerphone key, he set his phone on the nightstand. "My dad's coming to get me."

"Not that. I meant for fighting this injustice and proving your innocence."

"I . . . I don't know. Dr. Hightower said I could appeal, but she made it sound like I didn't stand much of a chance."

"So appeal. It's worth it. Cruz, this is what you've always wanted. All summer long, it was *Academy this* and *Academy that.* You can't give up. You were meant to be an explorer."

Cruz sighed. "Sometimes you can't be who you want to be. Sometimes you have to settle for who you are."

That sounded quite wise and mature, he thought.

There was a beat.

Then a grunt. "Talk about a load of stinky cheese."

Lani could always see right through him. It's what he loved about her. And hated.

"Besides," she said, "what you are is pretty awesome. You've been doing great on your missions."

"*Great?*" He coughed. "Have you forgotten how I got Sailor and me killed in the butterfly mission—"

"Have *you* forgotten how you helped Renshaw when he had his asthma attack and then went after the illegal loggers when no one else in your class did? You got bonus points."

"I got a B on the *Orion* mission—"

"You got a B *plus*, and you would have gotten an A if you hadn't stopped to help Emmett when he was seasick."

His head felt tight. He was getting a headache. Nobody could give him a headache faster than his best friend. "What's your point?"

"My point is it's not always about the grade. What you did for your teammates was more important than getting a good score, and if your professors can't see that then they're a bunch of warty fungus heads."

"She's right." Aunt Marisol was leaning in the doorway to the guest bedroom. "Well, except for the warty-fungus-head part."

"Uh . . . sorry, Dr. Coronado," squeaked Lani.

"You may not be an A-plus student on paper, Cruz," said his aunt, "but you're an excellent explorer. I guess there's no harm in telling you now—you're the talk of the faculty. Everyone is—was—quite impressed with you. Monsieur Legrand went on and on about your per-formance in the ARC, and Brent—Dr. Gabriel—was thrilled that you and Sailor tried something no one else had done on your very first training mission. Professor Benedict says you're an excellent photog-rapher with real potential."

"See?" said Lani. "You can't give up, Cruz. Not yet."

"I'm with her." Aunt Marisol's eyebrows went up. "It's your decision, of course."

Unsure, Cruz spun away. The buttercup yellow walls of the bedroom in his aunt's town house reminded him of Emmett's "contented" glasses. The cozy room was decorated with treasures his aunt had picked up on her travels: a stack of antique wooden English steamer trunks engraved with the date 1678, a crown of feathers from one of the tribes of the Amazon river basin, an Inuit whale baleen basket, a string of colorful Tibetan prayer flags, a *shekere* from Nigeria. Cruz had looked forward to starting his own treasure collection one day. He picked up the *shekere* and slid his palm along the blue-beaded netting that covered the outside of the dried gourd. The rattle instrument made a soft *wisha-wisha* sound. "*Fortes fortuna adiuvat,*" he murmured before turning back to his aunt. "What if I wanted to, just for argument's sake ... you know ...?"

"Fight this injustice and prove your innocence?" shouted Lani.

Cruz grinned. "Yeah, that. What then?"

"Okay!" Aunt Marisol rubbed her palms together. "We've got some detective work to do. First, we need to review the CAVE technical logs for those missions of yours that were altered. I'll touch base with the technicians tomorrow and request them so we can see for ourselves exactly what happened. We should also go through the mission videos. We might spot something, like another student tampering with something or acting suspicious." She tapped her chin. "The only problem is I don't have time to review the videos tomorrow and it would need to happen now. I'm in meetings all day when I don't have class. Is there someone, an explorer on your team, who you could trust to watch the clips?"

It had to be either Sailor, Bryndis, or Renshaw, since Emmett and Dugan were suspects.

"Renshaw," decided Cruz. "He's borrowed my notes enough times. He owes me a favor. Plus, he's a good guy."

"I'll contact him, and if he agrees, I'll set him up in my office where he won't be disturbed," said his aunt. "Once we know what we're dealing with and we have some good evidence on our side, we'll file the appeal."

"What about me?" asked Lani. "What can I do?"

Aunt Marisol took the words right out of Cruz's mouth. "Cross your fingers and toes that we find something to save Cruz."

ON MONDAY, CRUZ RETURNED to the sprawling Society campus with Aunt Marisol. It was weird being back there. It had only been a weekend, but he'd missed it. He missed his room, his teachers, his friends. Even Emmett. No longer a student, Cruz was not allowed inside the Academy. However, the museum was open to the public. He could hang out there for the day.

"Pick a civilization—Celtic, Viking, Maya, Roman, whatever catches your eye—and spend a few hours touring the wing," said his aunt as they parked in the lot behind the administration building. "Learn as much as you can about their society and be prepared to give me a full oral report after dinner tonight." She caught his expression. "What? You didn't think you were going to get out of learning just because you aren't in class, did you?"

Being related to a teacher could sure be annoying sometimes.

Aunt Marisol grabbed her coffee mug and they locked up the car. "Let's meet at five at Cool Beans—that coffee shop across the street from the Academy. Hopefully I'll have good news."

"Okay." With a wave, Cruz walked backward, watching until her yellow raincoat disappeared into the administration building.

The museum didn't open until nine, so Cruz waited in the snack bar off the lobby. He spotted three small tables tucked into the corner, took a seat at the one closest to the wall, and sipped his orange juice. When the museum opened, he was the first person inside. After a stroll through the Ancient Civilizations wing, Cruz settled on the Aztec Empire for his report. Aunt Marisol should like that.

Cruz moved from one display case to the next, reading the placards that described the ancient art, weapons, clothing, jewelry, and tools the Aztec people developed as they built the city of Tenochtitlan, which would later become Mexico City. He was reading a plaque next to a serpent-shaped lip plug made of obsidian when he saw, in the reflection of the glass, someone standing behind him. At first, he thought the person was politely waiting to view the artifact, but when Cruz moved to the next display case, his shadow moved with him. It was a man. His head was tipped down. That was all Cruz could see in the glass.

There was no one else in the exhibit. Cruz pretended to read the plaque next to a bust of Hernán Cortés, the Spanish conqueror who'd defeated the Aztec. Cruz had two choices: He could veer right and go through the doorway into the next exhibit or head left and take his chances with an exit door. To make sure he wasn't being paranoid, Cruz walked slowly to the next case. This one held a small tapestry depicting the war between Cortés's troops and the Aztec warriors. He heard the tap of soles against a stone floor. The man was still with him. *Now* he was worried.

Cruz took a couple of deep breaths, then bolted for the exit. He heard someone call his name. Racing down the stairwell, he could hear footsteps above. They matched his own frantic pace. Cruz flung open the door marked *L* and darted through the atrium. He passed the coffee cart and the info desk and was 10 feet from the main entrance when he saw the man in the snakeskin cowboy boots! He was outside, standing on the steps in front of the museum. Cruz banked right, directly into the gift shop. He zipped to the back of the store and hid behind a rack of postcards. He tried to think. Were there two men? Or had the one upstairs beaten Cruz to the front? No, he couldn't have made it outside that fast. There had to be two of them! Cruz was outnumbered. His heart pumping wildly, Cruz tried to get a grip. He waited inside the gift shop for another 10 minutes. When he dared to peer out the front window, he no longer saw the man in the cowboy boots, but he didn't want to risk it. He might be able to give them the slip if he left out a back door. Cruz hurried across the atrium and into the stairwell.

At the bottom of the stairs, he stopped to listen for footsteps. Hearing none, he cracked the basement door and saw the exhibit entrance to the Hall of Mammals. Cruz didn't see either of the men

chasing him, but he did spot a group of what looked to be sixth grad-
ers. He scurried out to join them as they went from the woolly mam-
moths of the North American wing to the elephants in the African
wing. He kept to the outer fringes, his eyes roving, searching every
nook and cranny for any sign of trouble. When the kids headed toward
the mineral and gem exhibit, Cruz hung back. He peered into the Hall
of Dinosaurs. It was empty. There was an exit door at the far end. He
estimated that he could be there in less than 30 seconds.

Cruz took off, weaving through the ancient skeletons of veloci-
raptors, spinosaurs, and triceratops. He was under the colossal head
of a *T. rex* when he felt an arm go around him, squeezing his shoulders
in a viselike grip.

"Ow! Let me go!" He struggled, but the man was much taller and
stronger than he was. Cruz caught a glimpse of snakeskin cowboy
boots.

"Enough games, kid."

Cruz was being dragged to the side of the exhibit hall. The man
punched through a door marked EMPLOYEES ONLY and shoved him into a
dim hallway. "March," he commanded, thrusting his palm into the small
of Cruz's back. Cruz stumbled down the hall 20 feet or so until his
hands found only cold concrete on all sides. It was a dead end. There
was nowhere for him to go.

His captor stepped under the dim glow of a lightbulb. Cruz watched
him pull a long gray scarf from his neck and stretch it tight in his
hands.

"You're … uh … Nebula?" Cruz said loudly, hoping someone would
hear.

"So it would seem."

"Why are you trying to hurt me?"

"Just following orders."

Cruz backed up until his spine hit cement. His heart began to pound
against his ribs. He knew there was no escape for him this time. "You
tried to kill me in Hanalei, didn't you?"

With a chuckle, the man gritted his teeth. "Don't worry. I'm a lot better on land."

Putting his arms up to defend himself, Cruz started to yell "Wait!" but the man lunged for him.

Thwunk!

His attacker collapsed at his feet. Cruz lowered his arms. He couldn't believe it! Cowboy Boots was out cold. Next to him stood a lanky man in a lab coat clutching a giant dinosaur bone.

"Jericho!" cried Cruz.

Jericho Miles tapped the bone against his palm. "These things really come in handy in an emergency."

"Am I glad to see you!" Cruz hadn't laid eyes on the Synthesis scientist since he had saved Emmett, Sailor, and him after the gas attack. His legs still wobbly, Cruz stepped over the unconscious man on the floor. "Thanks. If you hadn't come along—What *are* you doing here anyway?"

"In the right place at the right time, I guess," said Jericho, steering Cruz back down the corridor.

"I think he's got a partner," said Cruz. "Shouldn't we call the police?"

"We'll handle it."

"We?"

Two men in black nylon Synthesis lab suits appeared out of the shadows. One looked like a professional wrestler. The other was much thinner, yet he was the more threatening of the two. He held a hypodermic needle.

Cruz stiffened. "*You're* his partners!"

"No," said Jericho. "Easy there, Cruz. I don't know who that guy

is or what he wanted, but we're not with him. This is Lars and Maz, two of our lab techs. We're not here to hurt you."

Cruz stared at the metal needle inches from his face. "You sure about that?"

"We just need a blood sample."

"Thanks, but no thanks."

"It's not a request," said Jericho. "Look, I can have Maz sit on you, but it would be easier on all of us if you'd cooperate."

Cruz didn't move. The larger of the two men came toward him. Lifting a pair of thick hands, Maz grabbed Cruz under his arms and picked him up off the floor.

"All right, all right," cried Cruz, soaring upward. "You win."

Maz returned him to solid ground.

"Wise move." Jericho took the needle from Lars. "We'll make this quick and relatively painless."

Yanking his arms out of his jacket, Cruz began to roll up his right sleeve. "At least tell me what's going on?"

"Blood test. All Academy explorers must give blood before they can be cleared to travel."

Cruz stiffened. Jericho was lying. None of their professors had said anything about the explorers having to give blood before traveling. Taryn would certainly have mentioned it by now. Plus, international travel required vaccinations, which Cruz had already received back home, not blood tests. Something else was going on here.

"My . . . uh . . . boss said you were here this morning and I was to come get a sample—said you didn't like needles and to bring Lars and Maz along to make sure I got it," explained Jericho.

"Your *boss* forgot to tell you one thing," spit Cruz. "I'm not an explorer anymore. I've been expelled."

"What?"

"As of yesterday. Somebody hacked into the CAVE software and pinned it on me. I'm trying to figure out what's going on, but it's pretty hard when Nebula's trying to kill me, then you guys show up—"

"Nebula? Do you mean Nebula Pharmaceuticals?"

As if on cue, Cowboy Boots groaned.

A drug company! So Lani's research had hit the mark after all. Cruz remembered one of the companies on her list manufactured cold and flu medicine.

"Yeah, that's right," bluffed Cruz. "This guy is with Nebula Pharmaceuticals. You know them?"

Jericho shook his head, but the furrow between his eyebrows told Cruz differently. "Why would Nebula want to harm you?"

"That's what I'm trying to find out, among other things. Look, I know you work for the Synthesis," snapped Cruz. "And you still haven't answered my question: Why does *the Synthesis* want a blood sample from an explorer who no longer is one?"

Jericho stared at the needle in his grip. He didn't answer.

"Oh jeez, just get it over with and let me go," said Cruz, thrusting out his arm. He knew something was up, but Jericho wasn't talking. Cruz was tired. He turned his head, steeling himself for the sharp prick.

"Somehow, I know I'm going to regret this," moaned Jericho. Shoving up the sleeve of his lab coat, he jabbed the needle into the crook of his own arm. They watched the vial fill with maroon liquid. Jericho pulled the needle out and pressed a cotton ball into his elbow.

Cowboy Boots moved an arm. He was starting to come to. "You'd better get out of here, Cruz," said Jericho. "We'll have this guy arrested, but it won't stop Nebula, I'm afraid. I wish I could help more, but—"

"Thanks, Jericho. You saved my life." Cruz grabbed his jacket. "Again."

"Forget it. Get out of here."

"I owe you—"

"*Go!*"

Cruz went.

17

WHERE was she?

It was three minutes after five o'clock, and Cruz couldn't seem to keep his feet from jiggling or his hands from tapping the sides of his chair. He sat at a tippy table outside the coffee shop across the street from the Academy, though with his back turned to the street so that Emmett or any of the other explorers in his class would not see him.

He saw a flash of yellow sweep through his peripheral vision. The door opened and there she was!

Cruz could tell right away by Aunt Marisol's pinched face that the news wasn't good.

"Hi." She slipped into the wooden chair across from him and set her bag on the floor. "Did you get something to eat?"

"Not hungry. What did you find out?"

She pulled her arms out of her yellow raincoat. "The logs showed someone clearly changed the parameters of the program for your two CAVE missions." Aunt Marisol flung her coat over her chair.

"Unfortunately, in both instances, the IP address definitely came from your tablet. I'm afraid it's cut-and-dried."

"What about the videos?"

"Renshaw spent most of the afternoon going over them. Unfortunately, he didn't see anything out of the ordinary, other than the two glitches Dr. Hightower mentioned." She shook her head. "We came up empty . . . I'm sorry, hon."

Cruz felt himself deflate. He'd thought that having the truth on his side would somehow save him. It hadn't.

"We can still file the appeal, though," said his aunt.

"Without any evidence?"

She rubbed her forehead as if it might magically produce an answer. There were shadows under her eyes he hadn't seen before.

"So, I guess that's that, huh?" Cruz slid his thumbnail into a groove on the edge of the table. "I'll meet Dad's plane on Saturday and we'll turn around and go home."

Aunt Marisol let out a weary sigh. "I need a latte. Can I get you anything?"

He shook his head and she went to get in line.

Cruz absently glanced at the passing traffic. He still couldn't quite wrap his mind around the events of the past few days. One minute, he was hanging out with Emmett in the Mount Everest room and doing his homework with everything to look forward to, and the next . . .

He was here. In a coffee shop. With nothing to look forward to.

His aunt was back. She took a sip of her coffee. "I saw your holo-video ad. Taryn turned it in for you."

"Yeah?" Cruz tried to tell himself that it didn't matter if she liked it or not, but of course it mattered. He wanted her to be proud of him, even now.

He felt a hand gently cover his own. "It was wonderful. The way you talked about King Tut's tomb with such enthusiasm and energy, you reminded me of why I became an archaeologist all those years ago and why I can't wait to get out there again and . . ." Her voice dropped off.

Cruz fought back his emotions. "I know how much you wanted us to explore together, Aunt Marisol. I wanted it, too. I'm sorry—"

"You have nothing to be sorry for. It wasn't your fault. You couldn't help it if someone conspired against you."

"Do you think it was Emmett?"

"I don't know, Cruz. I just don't know." She drummed her cherry red nails on the table. "But so help me, if I ever find out..."

Cruz couldn't help grinning. Despite everything that had happened, she was still on his side, still fighting for him and protecting him. Like a mother. He knew he could always count on her. When their eyes met, when he looked into brown eyes like his own, Cruz knew he had kept the secret from her long enough. She deserved to know what he knew. He owed her that much. "Aunt Marisol, I need to tell you something."

"What is it?"

"It's about Mom... and something of hers she asked me to find."

"I'LL BET HE'S WEARING** the yellow-and-blue-zigzag shirt," Cruz said.

"We should have been able to spot that one as he landed." Aunt Marisol giggled. She tapped a scarlet fingernail against her chin. "I'll say he's in the kaleidoscope print."

"Didn't you get him that for Christmas?"

"I did," she said proudly.

They watched the passengers come through the terminal gate one by one—a woman cradling a baby, a bald man in a business suit with pants several inches too short, a family with matching peach-colored *I Love Hawaii* T-shirts.

"*Argh!*" cried Cruz as soon as he caught sight of the rayon shirt covered in a red-and-yellow diamond pattern. Aunt Marisol had won. Still, Cruz had never been happier to see one of his father's crazy shirts, even if it wasn't the one he'd bet on.

Once Cruz's dad saw them, his face lit up. Cruz hurried to him, wrapped his arms around his father's chest, and squeezed. As his tight hug was returned, Cruz exhaled. For the first time since leaving home, he felt safe.

His father leaned back to study him. "I sure have missed you.

I haven't had a slice of pepperoni and sausage since you left."

"Me neither."

"Marisol, how are we for time?"

Cruz wished they could stay one more night so the three of them could spend some time together but he knew his dad couldn't leave the Goofy Foot for long.

"We've got plenty—almost two hours before your return flight," she said. "Cruz is all checked in and has his boarding pass, so we're good there. Anybody hungry?"

"Starving," said his dad.

"Me too," said Cruz, flinging his backpack over one shoulder. He hadn't had much of an appetite since leaving the Academy, but was now suddenly ravenous.

Aunt Marisol took them to the grill near the main entrance that Cruz and Emmett had visited on Cruz's first day in Washington, D.C.

"A grilled cheese sandwich and a cup of tomato soup, please," Cruz said to the man behind the counter. Grilled cheese was his first meal in the nation's capital, so it seemed only right for it to be his last one, too.

Once they had their food, Cruz led the way to the same table where he'd sat with Emmett as they waited for his aunt to pick up Sailor. That first day seemed like ages ago. Cruz thought about how excited he had been to finally arrive in the city, and what a surprise it had been to see Emmett's glasses change shape and color! Cruz had liked his roommate from the start. It was too bad things had ended the way they did.

Cruz ate quietly while his dad and Aunt Marisol caught up on each other's lives. When he was done, he checked his messages. He had a text from Bryndis: *Cruz, I need to talk to you.* He texted her back: *What's up?* She didn't respond. She probably wanted to say goodbye. Bryndis hadn't been around when he'd left the campus.

After they finished eating, the trio walked around to kill time. They strolled past the rows of shops, stopping in at a few stores to browse, and down to the end of the terminal to watch the planes come and go. Finally, it was time to leave. At the security line, Aunt Marisol hugged

Cruz's dad. "Bye, big brother. Call once in a while." She turned to pull Cruz into an embrace. "And you, I'll see on your birthday."

"But won't you be on *Orion* with the . . . the . . . ?" The word stuck in his throat.

"I have a few days of vacation coming. It's not every year your only nephew hits his teens. I'll be there." She kissed him on the cheek. "Do you have Mell?"

He tapped the side pocket of his jacket.

"If you've left anything, let me know. I'll pick it up."

"And the journal?" he whispered.

"I'll talk to some people . . . do a little research . . . I can't promise anything."

He understood. "And, Cruz, promise me you'll fill your dad in, okay? You know I can't keep secrets from him."

Cruz grinned. Sometimes Aunt Marisol was too much like a mom.

"Okay. You're still going to send me coded postcards, aren't you?"

"You bet." She grinned. "It's tradition."

With one last bittersweet smile for his aunt, Cruz trailed his dad through the security line and to their gate. They boarded the plane and found their seats near the front of the cabin. His dad popped the overhead bin and slid Cruz's backpack inside. Settling into the window seat, Cruz fastened his seat belt. He looked out toward the terminal, searching for where he thought his aunt might be at the window. There! He spied her bright white jacket with the pink fringe trim. He waved, though he doubted she could see him.

In a few minutes, Washington, D.C., and the Academy would be in his past. It would be great to see Lani and all his friends again, of course, but it wasn't how he'd wanted to go home. True, someone had conspired against him, as Aunt Marisol had said, but a loss is a loss, no matter how it happens. And that, Cruz knew, would haunt him for a long time.

At least he'd have his aunt's postcards to look forward to. He hoped she'd make the next cipher a little tougher than the last one, but it was fun finding out that his mom's favorite book was *The Lion, the Witch and the Wardrobe.* He hadn't known that. The first thing he was going to do when he got home was reread the Chronicles of Narnia by C. S. Lewis. Yep, that's what he would do. Cruz leaned back.

Chronicles of Narnia. C. S. Lewis.

cslew.

Cruz bolted forward.

"What's the matter?" asked his dad.

He fumbled to release his seat belt. "Could you get my backpack?"

"They're about to close the doors."

"It'll only take a minute. I *have* to get into it. Please?"

With an annoyed sigh, his dad stood up. He opened the bin and brought down the pack. Cruz's hands shook as he unzipped the outer pocket. Could it be that simple? Cruz pulled out the small white notepad.

> *You are the only one I can entrust with this difficult mission. You are the only one I am certain can endure to the end. Find my journal. Find my life.*
> *Love, Mom*
> *pasc 823912 cslew*

"Come on, Dad," said Cruz, "we've got to get off the plane."

"Son, we're about to take off—"

"It's about Mom."

"Mom?"

"There's no time to explain. Please, Dad, trust me?" His eyes begged. "We have to go back to the Academy. *Now!*"

18

▶ **"...THE** message was in my birthday note all this time, except I didn't know it. I thought it was just a note and the swirls were just swirls, but then Emmett found a cipher on the back of the photo and we decoded the swirls, I mean, the symbols, and it turned out—"

"Whoa, whoa! Slow down, Cruz!" cried his dad from the front passenger seat of Aunt Marisol's hybrid. "You too, Marisol, or you're going to get us killed."

"Sorry," said his aunt, easing up on the gas pedal, "but the Academy library closes in fifteen minutes, and with this traffic, it's going to be close."

His dad looked at Cruz in the back seat. "All right, start again, but please use punctuation this time."

"Mom left me a message," Cruz said. "She wrote it in code on the birthday letter you gave to me. She left the cipher on the back of a photo of me she kept in her office. Aunt Marisol gave me Mom's stuff, and Emmett and I found the photo with the cipher. We decoded the message." He handed his father the notepad. "See? Mom says she kept a journal. She told me to find it."

"I had no idea—"

"I didn't know where to even begin looking," said Cruz. "I had no idea what those numbers and letters at the end meant. At first, I figured Mom hid the journal in the Synthesis, but Dr. Fallowfeld nixed that idea. He said everything was destroyed in the fire—"

"Dr. Fallowfeld?" broke in Aunt Marisol. "You didn't tell me you found Dr. Fallowfeld."

"He found me." Cruz saw a look pass between his aunt and his dad. "He said Nebula was behind Mom's accident. He warned me they would come after me, too. He practically ordered me to leave the Academy."

"When did he say this?" asked his dad.

"The day of orientation."

"And you're just telling us this now?"

"Dad!" Cruz rolled his eyes. "The point is, I thought the journal was gone forever. Then, when we got on the plane, I was thinking about Aunt Marisol's postcards. I remembered how she said she and Mom liked the Chronicles of Narnia series, and they used to use the books as ciphers when they passed notes at the Academy. That's when it hit me: Mom was trying to tell me where to find the book." Cruz stretched forward, tapping the pad in his father's hands. "Look, if you put a decimal between the three and the nine, it reads 823.912 cslew. It's the library's card catalog system. I bet that's where the series is located on the shelf in the Academy library, and if we look inside one of the books or in the boxed set we'll find Mom's journal."

"Not today you won't," said Aunt Marisol, craning her neck. "We're bumper to bumper here and still a good ten blocks from school."

His dad was frowning at him. "You really think it's there?"

"I do," said Cruz.

"We can run faster than this." Cruz's dad flung open his door. "Let's go, son."

Opening his door, Cruz hopped out of the car.

"Wait!" Aunt Marisol was waving her security card at him. "You'll need this to get in. I'll meet you there."

Cruz grabbed the card and took off after his dad, who was already sprinting down the sidewalk. About six blocks later, Cruz's legs started to give out. It felt like his lungs were seconds away from imploding, too. He had to stop.

His dad was at the corner. "Come on, Cruz!"

"I can't... take another step... I can't..."

"Yes, you can." His dad ran back to him. "We're almost there. You can see the roof of the Academy from here. We can make it."

Somehow, they *did* make it. Cruz dragged himself up the mountain that was the front steps of the Academy and waved the card in front of the sensor next to the security camera. The door opened and they raced inside, zipping through an empty lobby. Rounding the corner, Cruz prayed he'd see an open library door at the end of the long hall. He did! They weren't too late.

"Mr. Rook!" cried Cruz, speeding past the check-out desk.

A red head popped up. "Cruz?"

"Chronicles... of Narnia... where?"

"Narnia? Uh... that would be in fantasy... to the left... across from your favorite chair... but I'm about to close—"

"This will only take a sec!" Cruz flew into the maze of bookcases. He knew exactly which turns to take to navigate the way to his favorite thinking spot. Now it was his turn to yell: "Come on, Dad!"

"Right behind you."

Cruz zigzagged through the stacks, running to the rhythm of the numbers in his head.

823.912... 823.912... 823.912...

"This way, Dad," he called, throwing out verbal bread crumbs for his dad to follow. "Turn left at the magazines."

There! Just past the olive chair, he spotted the 800 to 8900 label on the end of the bookcase. Darting down the row, Cruz began scanning the spines. *801... 809... 814... 818... 821... 823... 823.325... 823.736... 823.946...*

"No!" he shrieked.

"What?" His dad pulled up beside him, panting.

"It's not here. It must be checked out."

"Don't panic. Look again."

Cruz did, but it was no use. "It's gone, Dad. It should be here between 823.736 and 823.946, but there's—" Above him, a gray box teetered on the wrong side of a bookend. Was it possible the series had been misshelved?

Cruz reached for a corner. The moment he saw the flowing mane of Aslan the lion he let out a whoop. He flipped the boxed set around to its open side and saw seven spines. None of them looked like a journal. Could it be inside one of the books? Cruz slid out *The Lion, the Witch and the Wardrobe*.

"Aunt Marisol said this one was Mom's favorite." Balancing the book flat on his palms, a wave of fear rolled through him. Cruz was scared to look. And he was scared not to. What if it wasn't here? No, it would be here. It *had* to be here.

Cruz eased open the cover. He turned one page. Then another. And another. He went faster and faster, until he had fanned through several chapters. There was no journal. No swirling symbols. Not even a new clue.

"Let's check the rest of the series," said his dad.

They split the remaining six titles between them. They found nothing.

Drained, Cruz sagged against the shelf. "I was so sure . . ."

"Sorry, son. It *was* a long time ago." Running his hand over the inside of the shelf, he blew the dust from his fingertips. "There's no telling what could have happened to it. It could have been lost or sold at a library book sale. They might have even recycled it."

Half of the lights above them went out. The library was closing.

"We'd better go," said his dad.

Defeated, Cruz shuffled back through the stacks. He supposed his dad was right. A hundred things could have happened to the journal in seven years. Still, wouldn't his mother have factored that in? She was a brilliant scientist. It seemed unlikely she'd have hidden her journal in a place where any explorer looking for a good book might discover it. Also, she wouldn't have taken the chance that it might be lost, sold, or recycled. If her journal was as important to her as her work, which she locked up every night, she'd want to put it someplace safe, someplace special, someplace where only a select few would have access to it...

Cruz grabbed his Dad's arm. "I know where the journal is."

"Where?"

His neck snapping back, Cruz spun in a circle until he saw the round, wooden door. He pointed to the fifth level of the rotunda. "There. Behind that door."

"What is it?"

"Special collections," said Mr. Rook, poking his head around the corner.

"Mr. Rook!" cried Cruz. "Can you take us to the rare book room, please?"

"I'd like to, but—"

"I know, I know, you're closing, but it'll only take a few minutes."

"It's not that. Don't you remember? Only explorers are allowed in the special collections room, and you...well, I'm afraid you..." He glanced at Cruz's bare wrist.

Cruz knew. He wasn't an explorer anymore.

"I *am* sorry," said the librarian.

Just last week, Cruz could have gone inside the special collections room. But not now. Cruz couldn't believe it. He was one door away from finding his mother's journal. He had come so close! He could not let it slip away. If uncovering the journal hinged on trusting Mr. Rook, then Cruz didn't see he had any other choice. He was going to have to tell the librarian exactly why he needed to get in that room.

"Mr. Rook, my mom was a scientist for the Society," said Cruz. "She died when I was five, but she left a letter for me. I only got it right before I came to the Academy. She asked me to find her journal. She said it was her life. I think—I know—it contains important things she wrote. Please," he begged. "It's the last request she ever made of me. I *have* to know if it's there."

The librarian stroked his red beard. "I could lose my job if it ever got out—"

"It won't," said Cruz. "I promise, it won't."

"We have only one Chronicles of Narnia book upstairs," said Mr. Rook.

Cruz had a feeling he knew which one it was. "*The Lion, the Witch and the Wardrobe?*"

Mr. Rook nodded. "All right. I'll take you up. Let me close first."

"Thank you," said Cruz's dad, holding out his hand. "I'm Marco Coronado."

"Malcolm Rook." The two men shook hands. "Hang tight, and I'll be right with you." While the librarian locked the doors and turned out the lights, Cruz texted his aunt to let her know what was going on. Soon, Cruz and his dad were climbing the spiral iron staircase behind Mr. Rook. The trio moved quickly up the side of the enormous rotunda from one level to the next to reach the curved catwalk on the fifth tier. Outside the round door, Mr. Rook pressed his thumb against a square screen, then entered a long numerical code. Cruz held his breath until he heard the latch give way.

Mr. Rook pressed on the handle and pushed the door open. He stepped inside. Turning on the lights, he motioned for Cruz and his father to enter, too, then closed the door behind them. Cruz was surprised. The half-moon-shaped room was nothing like the grand, modern library it was attached to. It was packed with antique bookcases, cabinets, and chests, with barely enough space for one person to slip between the various pieces of furniture. The walls were covered in old-fashioned coral-colored wallpaper with white roses. There were no windows. The place reminded Cruz of Aunt Marisol's attic, with one noticeable difference: The place was spotless. There was not a single cobweb or speck of dust anywhere.

"Oh, I know it looks like your grandmother's attic," said Mr. Rook, "but it's far from it, thanks to high-level security and state-of-the-art climate control. The temperature remains at a steady sixty-eight point five degrees Fahrenheit with twenty-five percent humidity. It's all carefully regulated and monitored to insure optimum conditions for our books, documents, photos, and maps."

Emmett would be happy to know that, thought Cruz. Warm from all the running, Cruz took off his jacket and hung it on one of the hooks by the door. On the other side of the door, a workbench held various tools. A mix of old-fashioned and high-tech gadgets lined the table: a set of knives and awls, assorted glues, an old book press, a microcomputer, and a mind-control camera. At the end sat a long white gizmo that resembled the handle of a solar-powered toothbrush. Cruz had no idea what *that* was.

"The book press belonged to Benjamin Franklin," said Mr. Rook.

"Cool." Cruz bent for a closer look. It was just two pieces of old, chipped wood held together with a black metal clamp with a handle for turning, but knowing it was once owned by Benjamin Franklin made it something special. Cruz thought about touching it, but didn't want to get in trouble. He was in enough trouble already.

"When it comes to special collections, I do all hologram, book, and document recovery and restoration myself," boasted the librarian.

"Impressive," said Cruz's dad.

Mr. Rook slid out the top drawer of a small oak chest to his left and took out several pairs of white cloth gloves. He handed a set to Cruz and another to his father. "Put these on. They'll keep the oils and dirt from your fingers from damaging the works. Everything in here is rare, old, expensive, irreplaceable, or all of the above."

"We'll be careful," said Cruz, putting on the gloves.

"The book you want should be in that first row in the tall bookcase with the glass doors. See it next to the mirrored armoire at the far end with the holo-videos?" Mr. Rook gestured about 20 feet ahead. "It'll be either on the third or fourth shelf. Be careful with it, please. It's a signed, first-edition copy in excellent condition. It's worth thirty thousand dollars."

"Thirty *thousand*?" gasped Cruz's dad.

"At least that. It was given to the Academy by Mr. Lewis himself."

Cruz's breath caught in his throat. If that was true, he doubted he would find his mother's journal there. She wouldn't cut out the pages of such a valuable book to hide her journal between the covers, would she? There was only one way to find out.

Cruz's stomach began doing backflips as he made his way down the narrow space between the furnishings. What if it wasn't here? When he reached the five-tiered bookcase, Cruz carefully opened the two glass doors and began scanning the spines on the third shelf. Cruz followed the authors' last names as they progressed in alphabetical order. It ended at the *J*'s. He had to go down on one knee to see the fourth shelf. As his eyes moved across the spines, his heart began to thump faster. *There! Lewis!*

"Got it!" Cruz pulled out the hardcover book wrapped in a light gray dust jacket.

Near the middle of the book, he noticed a white corner peeking out between the pages. It looked like an ordinary piece of scrap paper that someone had used as a bookmark. And yet...

Standing up, Cruz reached for the marker.

"Cruz, stay where you are," said his dad, his voice sounding odd.

Glancing up, Cruz saw that his father had his hands raised. Next to him, the Academy's head librarian was pointing something at his dad's ribs. Cruz recognized the long white tool from the workbench. "Hey, Mr. Rook," Cruz laughed nervously, "what's going on?"

"Ah, Cruz," replied the librarian. "It's really quite simple. I've been looking for something, and you've found it for me." Lifting his arm, he aimed at a spot above Cruz's head. A red laser beam shot from the device. In seconds, the burst had burned a hole clean through the ceiling. And the roof, too! Cruz could see daylight coming through the charred opening. The place smelled like someone was burning burgers on the grill. "So now that I have your attention here's what we're going to do." The librarian's usually cheerful voice had turned brittle. "Cruz, you're going to come back over here and hand me that book. Then the two of you are going to step away so I have a clear path to the door. Got it?"

Cruz was confused. "But ... but ..."

"Do what he says, son," instructed his dad.

"O-okay," said Cruz. He wasn't sure what was going on. Did Mr. Rook think they were here to steal something?

"Move," ordered the librarian.

Cruz started to hurry toward the two men.

"Slowly!" barked Rook.

Putting on the brakes, Cruz inched his way along the narrow path between the furniture. His mouth was dry, his hands starting to tingle. He felt a bead of sweat trickle down his back.

"That's far enough," said Rook when Cruz was at arm's length. The librarian took the book and placed it on top of the antique map cabinet next to him. He motioned with his weapon. "Marco, go stand with your son."

"Things always this exciting around here?" asked his dad.

"You have no idea," answered Cruz.

"Quiet, both of you. And keep your hands up." Rook gingerly opened the cover of the book and turned the pages with a gloved hand. Cruz and his dad remained still, watching page after page go by. Rook went faster and faster; the more pages he turned, the more careless he became. Suddenly, he stopped. Rook had reached the page with the white bookmark.

Cruz held his breath. Was there anything written on it?

Rook lifted out the three-by-three-inch square of scrap paper. He flipped the bookmark. "It's blank."

Cruz exhaled. "Another dead end."

"You're right about that." Rook raised his handheld laser.

"Hold on, there," burst Cruz's dad. "We're no threat to you, sir. You don't have to do this."

The librarian's eyes turned icy. "You are. And I do."

Cruz had seen that severe look before. He had a hunch. "Nebula!" snapped Cruz, and when the librarian stiffened, he knew his gut was right. "You're working for Nebula, aren't you?"

"What can I say? I've got a few secrets. And I need to make sure it stays that way." Rook's lip twisted. "Besides, it's *very* good money."

"It usually is," muttered Cruz's dad.

"Sorry, recruit." Rook flipped a switch on the laser, to increase the intensity of the pulse, no doubt. He took aim at Cruz. "You could have been a good explorer."

Cruz knew he should have been terrified, but he wasn't. Instead, a strange kind of calmness began to spread through him. It was like back home, when he'd toss his board into the surf, paddle out, and ride the waves. There are things you know about yourself deep inside, things no one has to tell you or teach you. You just know them. Staring past the weapon into Rook's hard eyes, Cruz lifted his chin and said what he knew. "I *am* a good explorer." Then he turned so he would be facing his father when he took his last breath.

19

CRUZ exhaled. Then inhaled. He was breathing! He glanced down. There were no holes in his body!

Beside him, Cruz's dad was alive and whole, too.

Rook had lowered the laser and was staring at the top of the map cabinet. "What the devil…?"

The bookmark was moving! Like a butterfly opening its wings, flaps were unfolding from the center of the square. The flaps multiplied and then began creasing themselves, as if someone was creating an origami sculpture, except no one was touching the paper! After dozens of lightning-quick pleats, a three-dimensional sphere made up of pointed triangles began to take shape. Once the pointy orb was complete, a pale orange light appeared at the tip of one of the paper triangles. The sphere rolled until the light faced Rook. A beam shot out. Starting at his head, the ray went smoothly and steadily down his body. When it reached his waist, it abruptly shut off. Ten seconds later, the sphere began to collapse—the triangles became flaps, and the flaps folded inward. It was like watching a video in reverse. Within seconds, the sphere was a flat, square piece of scrap paper once again.

"Remarkable!" said Rook. "I had no idea! I think this might be what you're looking for. Or should I say, what's looking for you." He waved the laser at Cruz. "Step on up and let's see, shall we?"

With a nervous glance at his dad, Cruz obeyed.

"No sudden moves or…" The librarian pointed his weapon at Cruz's father.

Cruz tapped the bookmark. As before, after about 15 seconds, the white paper transformed into a pointed sphere. Cruz stood still as the orange cone of light swept over him. He felt no heat. No discomfort. When the ray reached his stomach, it went out.

"See? Nothing. Nice try." Cruz spun away.

"Hi, Cruzer."

Cruz stiffened. It had been a long time since he had heard her call him that. Cruz turned. Drifting above the square was a three-dimensional holographic image of his mother. She looked the same age as she did in his beach holo-video, except her wavy blond hair was pulled back into a low ponytail. Over jeans and a long-sleeved white cotton shirt, she wore a gray cardigan sweater and belt with a brown leather buckle at the waist. The sweater looked familiar. Cruz felt a lump rise in his throat. He looked at his father, but his dad wasn't looking at him. He was gazing up lovingly at his wife.

Cruz approached the ghostly image. "Mom?"

"How are you, son?"

"I'm okay. It's been a crazy day, that's for sure. I had a hard time finding you."

"Sorry about that."

"It's all right, Mom." Cruz knew this was only a program, that she had prerecorded responses that were triggered by certain key words, such as "hard time finding you." Even so, she was talking to him and he was talking to her and for a moment he could pretend it was all real. "I … I … miss you, Mom." It felt so good to say that word out loud: "Mom." He wanted to say it over and over. *Mom. Mom. Mom.*

"I miss you, too," she said.

"Get going," growled Rook. "I don't have all night."

"Mom, I … uh … have questions," Cruz said to the image.

"I know," she answered. "Unfortunately, this program limits me in my responses. There's so much I want to say and not enough memory to say it." She grinned. "If you're seeing me now you must have decoded the message in your birthday letter. Congratulations, you have found my journal!"

"You mean, this is it?"

"Yes. I organized it into a digital robotic format that only you could access," she said.

"Why?" demanded Rook.

She did not respond.

"Ask her what's so important she had to hide it in a journal," Rook said to Cruz. When Cruz hesitated, the librarian waved the laser. *"Ask her!"*

"Uh ... Mom, why all the secrecy?"

"Several years ago, before you were born, I began doing research in the Synthesis with animal venoms. Science has taught us that the toxins snakes, scorpions, jellyfish, and thousands of other creatures produce to defend themselves have the potential to treat illness and injury in humans. Nebula Pharmaceuticals helped fund my research for a venom-based drug that showed promise in treating pain." She clasped her hands in front of her face. "However, the serum I developed did more than I anticipated. It not only alleviated the pain of the patient who took it, it also showed great promise in curing them of whatever was causing that pain—the common cold, a broken leg, arthritis, kidney disease, even the last stages of cancer. The serum's regenerative properties on the cellular level were nothing short of miraculous."

"Wow," said Cruz, his dad, and Rook in unison.

"Of course, the last thing a pharmaceutical company making billions of dollars selling drugs wants is for humanity to never need those drugs," continued Cruz's mother. "Nebula demanded I destroy the serum and the formula. Under pressure, I agreed, but I knew that wouldn't be the end of it. As long as I was alive, as long as I had knowledge of the serum, my life was in jeopardy. I wanted to tell your father but doing so would have put him and you in grave danger, too."

Cruz glanced at his father. Mesmerized, his dad had tears in his eyes.

"I knew Nebula was watching me, monitoring my every move," she continued. "I couldn't let such an important discovery be lost to history, but I couldn't record it either, not on any computer, even one at home. That's when the idea came to me. It was so simple, really.

"I requested to travel with the explorers on *Orion* as a research mentor for the older students. Before we left port, I laser-engraved the formula onto a piece of black marble and split the stone into eight fragments. During our voyage, I hid the pieces in different places around the globe." Beside her appeared a floating collage of handwritten notes, directions, illustrations, maps, and coordinates.

"If you choose to find the pieces of my formula, this journal will guide you," she said. "Each time you find a fragment of the stone, show it to me—this image that's standing in front of you. If it's a genuine piece, it will unlock another clue. For security purposes, the clues will be coded and many will contain hints you must decipher. Once you have assembled all eight parts, you'll receive further instructions."

She turned to face him. "Since you were born, I knew you were destined to do great and important things. You may have your father's good looks, but you have my sense of adventure." Her lips straightened. "I won't lie. It will be dangerous. Nebula may try to stop you, even hurt you. Others may, too. The Synthesis supported my work, but sided with Nebula over the destruction of the formula. I don't know, at this point, if the Synthesis is to be trusted. If you'd rather not attempt it, I'll understand. In fact, I'll be a bit relieved, and I'm sure your dad will, too. Destroy this journal, don't look back, and live a happy life, knowing I am, and always have been, proud of you. Take as much time as you need to consider my request," said his mom. "This is a great responsibility, and you must decide if it is worth the sacrifices you will no doubt have to make. The choice is yours."

Cruz looked into his dad's glistening eyes and knew in an instant what his answer would be. "Mom, I don't have to think about it. I'll do it."

"Somehow, I knew you'd say that. Do your best to find my formula, son, and share my life's work with a world that desperately needs it."

Cruz swallowed hard. "Where do I start?"

"To find the first piece of the serum formula, dig through our family memories. I know you can do this. You can do anything you set your mind to. I'll see you soon."

"Wait!" Cruz fell against the map cabinet beneath her image. "That's it? That's the clue?"

"You have all you need to know to begin. I love you, Cruzer. Never forget, you are an extraordinary human being." Lifting a hand, she disappeared.

Within seconds, the sphere transformed back into a flat white bookmark. Rook pounced on it. "Nebula is going to want this." He stuck it in his back pocket, then nudged Cruz with the laser. "They're going to want you, too, recruit. You heard your mother. You're the key to unlocking all of this."

"I don't think so," said Cruz's dad. "This has gone far enough, Rook. My son isn't going anywhere with you."

"No?" Rook lifted his weapon.

"Whoa, whoa, whoa!" cried Cruz, stepping in front of the laser. He had an idea. "I'll go with you, Mr. Rook. I'll help Nebula find all the pieces of the formula and I won't be any trouble, but they have to promise to *never* harm my dad, my aunt, or anyone I care about."

A little vein in Rook's neck began to vibrate as he considered it. "All right. Your family won't be hurt. You have my word."

"For whatever that's worth," murmured Cruz's dad.

"Get your coat," Rook ordered Cruz.

Cruz scooted past the librarian. In one quick motion, he snatched the Narnia book off the map drawer and tucked it against his hip. At the door, he lifted his jacket off the hook. Cruz rustled the sleeves to mask his whisper of "Mell, on."

The weapon still trained on Cruz's dad, Rook backed up until he was next to Cruz. He opened the door and nodded to Cruz. "You go first. I'll be right behind you. Don't try anything."

"*Fortes fortuna adiuvat,*" murmured Cruz.

"What did you—"

Cruz flung the book at Rook, who ducked, but not fast enough. The novel smacked him in the face.

Cruz saw a flash of red. "Mell, defense mode!" he cried. "Target: man holding the laser. Mell, go!"

The honeybee drone shot out of Cruz's pocket, zeroed in on Rook, and began poking the librarian. She zipped up and down, left and right, stinging him on the shoulder, the face, the head, the chest, then back to the face. Mell was moving so quickly Cruz lost track of her, but he knew she was hitting her mark by Mr. Rook's yelps.

"Ouch! Ow! Ow!" Rook tried to fight off the drone, but she was too fast for him.

Reeling back, Rook tripped on the doorjamb behind him. He smashed into the railing of the catwalk, dropping the laser. His foot skidded through the opening between posts. He tried to keep his body from going through, too, but couldn't. Sliding over the side, Rook flailed his arms, frantically groping. One hand caught the bottom of a post. He brought the other hand up. Cruz and his dad charged forward. Rook was dangling 50 feet above the library floor, clinging to two metal posts. And one of them was bending.

Cruz clamped his hands around the librarian's left wrist. His dad took the right wrist. "Set your feet!" his dad shouted. Crouching, Cruz got into a wide stance. "Now pull!" ordered his dad.

Cruz heaved with all his might, but gravity was not on his side. Now deadweight, Mr. Rook was pulling *him* over the edge. Cruz could feel his grip slipping.

"Let me go," pleaded Rook. "Just let me go."

With a massive grunt, Cruz arched his back and pulled. It felt like his knees were going to explode.

"That's it," he heard his dad cry. "We've got 'im." With one big yank, they managed to drag Rook up onto the catwalk.

Cruz and his dad collapsed against each other.

"I can't believe I almost…" Rook looked at Cruz and his father in astonishment. "I can't believe you…"

"Cruz! Marco!" Aunt Marisol was coming through the main door of the library with Taryn.

"Up here," yelled Cruz's dad, getting up on his knees to wave. "Call security." To Cruz, he ordered, "Stay here, son. I'll get the laser."

Rook didn't try to run. He cowered in a heap against the wall, catching his breath. As several security guards raced up the steps to the catwalk, the librarian stretched an arm toward Cruz. "Here." He held out the paper that was Cruz's mother's journal. "This belongs to you."

Cruz took it. He was feeling tired, suddenly—light-headed and a bit disconnected from reality. Something, somewhere was starting to throb, but he couldn't tell where. It was as if he were in a dream and wanted to wake but couldn't. "Mell, come here." The bee drone came to land on his shoulder. "Good job, Mell … good job. Turn off."

That's when Cruz saw the blackened hole in his right sleeve. Beneath its tattered remains, he saw a smoking white hole surrounded by fiery red skin. He'd been hit by Rook's laser blast.

Cruz closed his eyes to shut out the growing wave of pain.

It didn't work.

20

"YOU WERE very lucky," said Dr. Ainsley. "The laser just grazed you. Laser burns can be serious. But a laser of this strength..." He paused, shaking his head. "A few millimeters to the right and it would have burned a hole right through you."

Cruz knew.

The emergency room doctor finished dabbing antibiotic cream on Cruz's wound. "Okay, you're all set. You'll have some pain and more blistering over the next few days," he explained, washing his hands. "The nurse will be in to bandage your arm. Be sure to take it easy. Stay hydrated and get some rest."

"I will."

Dr. Ainsley left the cubicle, flinging the curtain into place behind him.

Cruz glanced at his dad, sitting in a chair opposite the bed. "Where did Aunt Marisol go?"

"I sent her to pick up your prescriptions and get something to eat. She was looking a bit pale."

No wonder. With one eye closed, Cruz glanced at the divot in his arm. The shiny white skin that hadn't peeled away in pink strips was beginning to blister and ooze. The wound was still throbbing, though not nearly as much as it had an hour ago. Cruz could hardly believe the Academy librarian, the man who was always so friendly and helpful to the explorers, had come so close to killing them. "I never would have thought Mr. Rook was capable of this..."

"Anyone is capable of anything," his dad said warily.

"Mr. Rook is going to tell Nebula about Mom's journal, isn't he?"

"Probably, but maybe sitting in that jail cell will give him some time to think about the choices he's made so far, and the ones he could make in the future."

"At least he gave me the journal." Reaching for his back pockets, Cruz let out a shriek. "Dad! The journal!"

"It's okay." His dad patted a zippered pocket on the front of his jacket. "Safe and sound."

Cruz clutched his heart. That was a relief.

Next to the bed, the blue privacy curtain was swaying. Cruz could make out two figures. "Dad!"

His father jumped up. "Who's there?"

"Cruz? Are you here?" came a soft Icelandic accent.

"Bryndis?"

A fair blond head appeared. "The nurse said it wasn't too serious. She let us come back. Of course, I did tell her we were your cousins." Bryndis slid the curtain aside to reveal the other figure.

"Dr. Hightower!"

The Academy president's face was almost as white as her hair. "Are you all right, Cruz? We heard you'd been shot."

"Not *shot* shot," Cruz was quick to correct her.

"I got hit by a laser."

Peering at Cruz's fried arm, Bryndis winced. "That's bad enough."

"The doctor was just in," said Cruz's dad. "We should be able to take him home soon."

"Thank goodness," sighed the Academy president. "We got here as quickly as we could. Bryndis was with me in my office when we got the news. And, funny thing"—she let out a small chuckle—"we were discussing you, Cruz."

"Me?"

"Bryndis brought something rather interesting to my attention."

Dr. Hightower motioned to the girl standing next to her. "You want to tell him?"

With a shy grin that revealed a dimple on each cheek, Bryndis flipped a lock of hair behind her ear. "When I heard about . . . what happened, Cruz, I knew it had to be a mistake, so I decided to do a little investigating on my own. I went back and looked at the team videos, you know, from our CAVE missions—"

Cruz put up a hand. "Thanks, but we did that already—"

"So you saw it, too?"

"Saw what?"

Bryndis opened her tablet and brought up a video. "This clip is from our butterfly mission, when we stopped to rest because Renshaw was having trouble with his asthma. Watch." As Cruz, his dad, and Dr. Hightower circled her, she hit the arrow to play the video.

"I'm . . . all right," huffed Renshaw. "I just need a second. I have asthma . . . the altitude can get to me sometimes. My family . . . we're into sports, so I'm used to it. I've got my inhaler with me if it gets worse."

"Did you bring water?" Cruz heard himself ask.

Renshaw shook his head and took the bottle Cruz offered him.

"Thanks." Renshaw drank some water. "You guys can go on ahead. I'll catch up with you at the clearing."

"No," said Cruz. "We're gonna stay together."

"Okay. Thanks."

Bryndis stopped the video. "Did you hear it?"

Cruz shook his head.

"Renshaw told us he'd catch up with us at *the clearing*. We'd been hiking up a steep trail with nothing but forest around us. How did he know there was a clearing ahead?"

"I don't know." Cruz shrugged. "Lucky guess? Or maybe his brother told him?"

"That would be a serious violation of CAVE guidelines," interjected Dr. Hightower. "As you know, to prevent anyone from gaining an unfair advantage, explorers are never to discuss missions with anyone outside their teammates or professors."

"There's more," said Bryndis. "This one is from our *Orion* mission. Dr. Benedict said it was a new program and we were the first team ever to do it, remember? This clip is right before we got on the ship." Bryndis tapped her screen and the video began to play.

"Bon voyage, explorers!" Professor Benedict faded from view.

"I hope they have hot chocolate on the ship," said Sailor.

"It would technically be virtual cocoa." That was Emmett.

"I've got dibs on Ridley for my news story," said Dugan.

"I'll take the research labs," said Bryndis. "If that's okay with everyone else."

"I think I'd like the observation deck," said Sailor.

"Good choice," said Renshaw. "You'll probably see a lot when we go through the Bering Strait."

Bryndis paused the clip. "Did you catch it?"

This time, Cruz had spotted the error! He gasped. "Professor Benedict never told us where the ship was headed. Renshaw couldn't have known we were going through the strait unless—"

"He'd peeked at the program," finished Bryndis with a proud smile.

Cruz slapped his head. Didn't it figure? The *one* person he'd picked to try to save him was the very culprit they were after! How could Renshaw have done something so terrible? And to him? Cruz had thought they were friends. He shook his head in disbelief.

Cruz's dad turned to the Academy president. "What happens now?"

"I've already contacted Renshaw's parents. He's admitted he altered the programs. He said he had nothing against you, Cruz. That he used your tablet because it was the easiest to gain access to—something about getting around our security protocols to plant a virus in your tablet when you emailed him some of your class notes."

"Of course!" cried Cruz, remembering. "The dancing chipmunk."

Everyone was looking at him oddly.

"Anyway," said Dr. Hightower, "the virus allowed him to use your IP address to hack into the CAVE server. He said he was sure no one would ever discover the hack and you'd never get in trouble; but, of course, this *is* the Academy and we *did* notice. It was the virus that caused the flickers that our faculty and techs found. When they went in to try and fix the problem, they discovered what you—I mean, *he*—had done."

Cruz's disbelief was slowly turning to anger. Renshaw had to have known that someone *sometime* would discover the hack and that Cruz would take the blame for it, hadn't he? Maybe he hadn't. Maybe he didn't care.

She wrung her hands. "Renshaw is an exceptionally intelligent student. Sadly, he chose not to use his brilliance in a manner befitting Explorer Academy. He has been expelled. I had just sent for Bryndis and was telling her all this when we heard about Rook in the library."

"I don't get it," said Cruz. "Renshaw didn't need to cheat. He was doing well in school."

Bryndis bit her lip. "Maybe really well isn't good enough when your brother is a North Star award winner."

"Or you're a perfectionist," mumbled Cruz, remembering Emmett's warning.

Emmett!

Oh, man, did he owe Emmett an apology the size of Mount Everest. His roommate hadn't cheated after all. Somehow, in his heart, Cruz had always known Emmett couldn't have done it. He should have listened to his heart instead of his head.

Dr. Hightower was clearing her throat. "Cruz, with the board's unanimous support, I'm pleased to tell you that you are hereby reinstated at Explorer Academy with all traces of this entire incident to be permanently wiped from your record. I'd also like to extend my sincere apology for unjustly accusing and judging you."

Cruz didn't know what to say. He certainly hadn't expected this. "Thanks, Dr. Hightower!"

"If you're feeling well enough, and your father will allow you to return, you may board *Orion* with your classmates on Monday," said Dr. Hightower.

Monday?

"I'm ready to come back to the Academy right now, Dr. Hightower!" he blurted.

"Hold on, son." His father stepped in. "The doctor recommends a few days' rest." He looked at Dr. Hightower. "Also, before I can give permission for Cruz to return, I need to speak with you about the ... situation that happened today and what it means for Cruz."

"Naturally. The safety of all of our explorers is our top priority."

The nurse came in to dress Cruz's wound. His dad, Dr. Hightower, and Bryndis left the cubicle to give them privacy. "Your burn is already looking better," said the nurse.

Cruz had to admit the pain had decreased. It now felt like a wasp's sting.

The nurse carefully placed a large bandage over the wound. "Keep this on for a couple of days. And let us know if your pain gets worse, the wound changes color, or you run a fever." She helped him get into the shirt his dad had dug out of his luggage. "There you are, all ready for your girlfriend."

Did she mean Bryndis? Cruz felt his face flush. "She's not my girlfriend."

"No? Too bad. She's awfully cute, and she certainly has eyes for you." Bryndis? A crush on him?

He doubted it. She was cute and smart and funny, but they were just teammates. Just friends ... Weren't they?

"WE'VE GOT PIZZA!"

Aunt Marisol sang out, coming through the door.

Cruz hoped it was pepperoni and sausage with extra cheese. He shut off the TV in his aunt's living room.

"Pepperoni and sausage with extra cheese." She zipped past him. *Yes!*

"We picked up a few other things, too," added his dad. Cruz heard him shut the front door of the town house.

Cruz hoped one of those things was ice cream.

His dad came into the living room carrying a canvas bag filled with groceries. "Do you know that nobody in this town has ever heard of macadamia nut ice cream? I had to settle for rocky road. Oh, and these guys…"

"Surprise!" cried Sailor and Emmett, rushing in.

Cruz couldn't believe it! He hopped off the sofa to throw his arms around Sailor.

"Careful, son," said his dad.

"It doesn't hurt," said Cruz, which was true. It was only yesterday that he'd been burned, but he felt fine.

His dad headed into the kitchen with the groceries.

Releasing Sailor, Cruz turned to his roommate, who was pretending to study an 18th-century Chinese white porcelain vase on the fireplace mantel. "Emmett, I'm really sorry. Sailor told me I was wrong. I should have listened to her. I should have known you'd never do anything like that."

"Cheat? Or blame you for something I did?"

"Both." He winced. "I am really, really sorry."

Emmett gave him a sideways glance. "It's okay. You'd just been expelled. You were pretty upset. I'd have probably done the same thing in your place. It was an easy conclusion to jump to."

"I promise, I won't ever make that leap again."

"Good. 'Cause you almost broke my emoto-glasses!"

"Sorry! And I . . . I'd understand if you didn't want to be roommates on *Orion*."

"Too late." Emmett's egg-shaped glasses were turning from spring green to buttercup yellow. "I already signed us up to room together."

Cruz crossed his fingers. "Let's hope that seasick band of yours really works."

Aunt Marisol called them to dinner. Sitting around his aunt's mosaic kitchen table with his family and friends, talking and laughing and eating, Cruz felt lucky. Content. Loved. No matter where in the world he traveled or what amazing things he saw, Cruz was sure nothing would make him happier than he was right now. Cruz had three slices of pepperoni and sausage pizza with extra cheese. Skinny-as-a-toothpick Emmett ate four. That guy was a bottomless pit!

After dinner, Cruz took his friends to the guest bedroom and told them about everything that had happened since they'd discovered the cipher on the back of the photograph. Cruz set the digital journal on the dresser. As the page began its metamorphosis, Sailor jumped up. "Sweet as!" she cried. "It's like something Emmett would have invented."

"I wish," said Emmett, daring to touch one of the sphere's points.

They quieted down once Cruz's mother appeared. When the video ended, Cruz told them, "I'm going to do it. I'm going to try to find the pieces of my mom's formula. Dad agreed to let me go, though it took a little convincing."

Truth was, it took a lot of convincing. Dr. Hightower had promised to beef up security on the ship and to let Cruz's dad visit whenever he wanted.

"Aunt Marisol is going to help coordinate our curriculum locations with the clues we decipher. Well, we're going to try to get as close as we can, anyway." Cruz watched the sphere deconstruct itself. "Here's the hard part. We can't tell anybody what we're doing—not our teachers or the other explorers, not even our teammates. It would put them in danger, too. Only *Orion*'s captain, Captain Iskandar, and Aunt Marisol will know we're hunting for the formula."

Emmett swallowed hard. "We?"

"You guys are going to help me, aren't you?"

"Absolutely," said Sailor.

Emmett's glasses were pulsing yellow and lime. He was in!

"Once we set sail on *Orion,* my dad's going to fly back to Kauai," said Cruz. "Mom told me the first clue was in a memory, so we think it's likely to be in some of our stuff at home. Dad's going to look for it."

Sailor glanced up at the space where the image of Cruz's mother had been only moments before. "That holo-video sure seems real. It must have been a shock to see your mom after all this time, huh?"

"It was a surprise," said Cruz, "but not a shock. I *have* seen her. I mean, I do see her. I have another holo-video. I left it at home, though. We're all at the beach together—Mom, Dad, and me. I've watched it a billion times. I know every word by—" Cruz froze.

"Heart?" offered Sailor.

"It can't be a coincidence." Cruz grabbed his phone, wildly tapping the screen. "It just can't."

Emmett and Sailor were staring at him, waiting for an explanation.

"My mom said the exact same thing in the clue that she does in my beach holo-video. *You can do anything you set your mind to.*" Cruz let out a laugh. "It's been sitting in my room this whole time!"

"Aloha," said the voice on his phone. "What's up?"

"Lani, I need a favor."

CRUZ TROTTED DOWN THE PIER at National Harbor
Marina ahead of his dad, his backpack punching his shoulder
with every joyful step. Cruz loved the way the wood creaked
and swayed beneath his feet. It was good to be close to water—*real
water*—again. Cruz passed the crew loading food, equipment, and
other supplies into the cargo hold of the ship. Shading his eyes with a
hand, Cruz tipped his head back. The midday sun glinted off the windows of the white decks stacked above the dark blue hull. This *Orion*
was exactly like the one in the CAVE, and yet it was nothing like it. Cruz
had a feeling that's how it was going to be from now on. Simulation
training could only take you so far; then you had to face the world on
your own. He was ready.

"Got everything?" asked his dad, catching up to him at the gangway.

"I think so," said Cruz, touching the brown leather lanyard that
hung from his neck. Tucked inside his T-shirt, at the end of the tether,
was the first fragment of black marble containing his mother's formula. Cruz's hunch about his mom's first clue had been right. He'd had
it all along.

"Are you sure you want me to unscrew the base?" Lani had asked,
once she'd located the mini projector in Cruz's room. "What if I ruin it?
You love this video."

Cruz knew damaging his beach video was a possibility, but it was a
chance he had to take. Gritting his teeth, he'd said, "Do it."

And she had. Lani separated the circular bottom cap from the rest
of the base, and a small black stone had dropped into her palm. She'd
sent the rock to him via overnight mail.

"Well done," said his mother's image when Cruz had held the fragment up for her inspection. "This is a genuine piece. You have unlocked
a new clue. Travel north to the land of skrei and heather, Odin and Thor.
Seek the smallest speck, for it nurtures Earth's greatest hope." Next

to her, the outline of what appeared to be a worn and jagged arrow-head appeared. "If you run into trouble, go to Freyja Skloke. Good luck, son!"

Cruz raced to scribble down everything she'd said. He knew Odin and Thor were Norse gods, so she must want him to go to a Nordic country. But which one? Denmark, Norway, Sweden, Finland, or Iceland? On the plus side, the explorers were already scheduled to head north to Newfoundland on *Orion* for the first leg of their expedition. Cruz had no idea what the ancient spear tip was supposed to signify, but he had time to figure it out and family and friends to help him. His dad and Aunt Marisol had both been stunned to discover he'd found the first piece of the formula so quickly. He also knew they were worried about him seeking the rest of the cipher, especially with Nebula still out there.

Cruz looked up at his father. The same squiggly lines that had etched their way across his brow when he'd seen the stone fragment were back. "I'll be all right."

"I can't protect you at sea. What if—"

"There's extra security on the ship. Plus, Aunt Marisol will be there. Plus, *plus,* I'll follow all the rules. I'll be careful."

"I'm sure you will, but—"

"Dad, you know I have to go. When will I ever have this chance again?"

His dad's worry lines smoothed a bit. "If a task is too hard or you can't find a piece of the stone, don't push it—"

"I won't."

"You can always return later. There's no time limit."

"I know."

Speaking of time . . .

Cruz tilted his head toward the ship. "I'd better go."

They hugged.

"I love you, son."

"Love you, too, Dad." Cruz took the suitcase his dad handed him and marched up the gangway. At the top of the ramp, he turned and waved. His dad lifted a hand.

"I can do it, Dad," Cruz said quietly. "You'll see."

Emmett met him in the atrium on the main deck. "I found our cabin. We're up on the second deck."

Cruz followed his roommate up the wide curving staircase in the center of the atrium. They'd been assigned to cabin 202; like their old dorm, it was a corner room.

"I took the bed by the closet, if that's okay," said Emmett, suspiciously eyeing the porthole.

"Sure." Cruz set his suitcase and backpack on the floor. There was something on his bed. A package! Cruz picked up the padded yellow envelope and tore off the end. Inside was a rectangular box wrapped in turquoise paper and tied with a white ribbon. A small card was tucked under the ribbon. Cruz opened the present. It was a square sleeve, about four inches on each side, made of a thin yet sturdy material. He rubbed his thumb against it. It felt like fabric, however, he could not bend it. Cruz slipped a finger into the open end of the sleeve. There was nothing inside. Strange. He reached for the card.

I made this to protect your mom's paper journal. It's bulletproof, waterproof, explosion-proof, and even Cruz-proof. I could have done better if I'd had more time.

Aloha, Lani

Cruz laughed. Leave it to Lani to know what he'd need and then whip it up like some kind of tech chef. He opened his backpack and took his mom's origami journal out of the sandwich bag he'd packed it in with two pieces of cardboard. Cruz slid it into its new protective sleeve. It was a perfect fit!

"Hey, guys!" It was Dugan, Zane, and Ali.

"Dugan and I are right next door, and Zane is just across the hall," said Ali.

"Just like back at the dorm," said Emmett, "Except…"

They nodded solemnly. Renshaw wasn't here. Not having him around was going to take some getting used to. He may have made a bad choice, but he wasn't a bad guy. Not really. He'd let the pressure get to him. Cruz knew it could have happened to any of them—even him. Every second Cruz was on *Orion,* his anger at Renshaw dissolved a little more. Renshaw McKittrick would never be an explorer now. The person he had hurt most in all of this was himself.

Wooooot!

It was the ship's horn.

"Good afternoon, gentlemen." Taryn breezed into the cabin.

Cruz looked down, eager to welcome the white pup that always trailed her, but she was alone. His heart sunk. "Didn't you bring—"

"You're the hundredth person to ask me that. I think you explorers would rather have Hubbard aboard than me!"

Everyone laughed.

"Relax," said Taryn. "Hubbard's here. He's in my cabin while I attend to business, which is to inform you that we are about to set sail, so please report to the third aft deck to wave farewell to your families. Except you," she said to Cruz when he would have followed his friends. "Cruz Coronado, you didn't stop at the purser's desk."

"Was I supposed to?"

"You were. Technically, you're a new explorer. I have to check you in." Taryn pulled out the desk chair for him, then took a seat opposite in the overstuffed white chair with anchors printed on it. She reached into a red-and-white-striped tote bag. "This is your digital notebook, now virus free." She handed him his old tablet computer. "You'll use it for your assignments, training sessions, and field notes. It also contains your orientation video, school rules, and shipboard map. Review and memorize, please."

"Taryn, I already know——"

"Don't interrupt. Left wrist, please."

Cruz held out his arm. She snapped the gold band on him, and as he watched it slowly mold to his wrist, he couldn't help smiling. It felt good to have it back on.

"This is your passkey," teased Taryn. "Hold it up to a security cam and it will get you into anyplace explorers are allowed on the ship."

"Are you through?"

"I believe so," she said with a smirk.

He felt the ship's engine rumble beneath them. "We're moving!"

Flying out of their chairs, they hurried out to the wraparound veranda attached to the stateroom. Cruz searched the crowd on the dock. "There's my dad!" His father was standing next to the president of the Academy. Cruz was surprised. "Dr. Hightower isn't coming with us?"

"No," said Taryn. "She'll fly in to check on us from time to time, but she has to keep the home fires burning."

Waving like mad, Cruz turned to Taryn. "Do you have anyone seeing you off?"

"Nope—free as bird."

The pair kept waving long after anyone onshore could see them. Only when the ship went around a bend and they lost sight of the marina did they drop their arms and go back inside the cabin.

"Don't forget, there's a meeting for all explorers in the conference room on the third deck at two p.m." Taryn slung her tote bag over one shoulder. "Will you remind Emmett?"

"Yep, but I'm sure Emmett knows."

"Don't be late or you might miss the surprise."

"Surprise?" His ears perked up. "What is it?"

"They don't call it a surprise for nothing."

"You can tell me, Taryn. I promise I won't breathe a word to another living soul." Cruz put his hand over his heart. "Above all, honor."

Taryn wagged her finger at him. "Nice try."

Cruz thought so. Flinging his suitcase on the bed, he began to unzip it.

At the door, Taryn turned. "Oh, and, Cruz?"

"Yes?"

"Welcome to the Academy."

THE TRUTH BEHIND THE FICTION

Many of the ideas in Explorer Academy were inspired by real National Geographic explorers at the forefront of cutting-edge research. Their discoveries mean features like Emmett's color-changing, shape-shifting glasses and Cruz's mom's robotic origami journal may not be as far-fetched as you might think.

- **MATERIALS ARCHITECT SKYLAR TIBBITS** has already developed 4-D printing—which adds the concept of time and assembly to 3-D-printed objects. In other words, after a 3-D object is printed, it can then assemble itself on its own! To do this, Tibbits uses materials and geometry to construct an object that will fold and unfold in certain ways. Then he adds a source of energy—whether it's heat, gravity, magnetics, or something else—to initiate an interaction that causes the material to go from one state to another. In *The Nebula Secret*, we see this happen when Cruz's mom's journal unfolds at Cruz's touch. But the future of this technology is endless: Imagine clothes, shoes, furniture, and even cars that can change structure and adapt to their surroundings.

- **ALTHOUGH THE AUGMENTED REALITY CHALLENGE (ARC)** may be a fictitious game, the ability to layer computer images over actual surroundings is real. The technology has the potential to take us far beyond mere fun and games. Imagine firefighters going into a smoke-filled building aided by headgear that offers an overlay of the floor plan, or students watching a historic event unfold at the actual location where it occurred. From helping us locate restaurants on a busy street to stars in the night sky, scientists say that augmented reality could one day be as common as surfing the net.

- **CRUZ'S MAV DRONE HONEYBEE, MELL,** might sound like a thing of science fiction, but scientist Robert Wood leads a team of engineers who have already developed micro-robotic insects! Smaller than a quar-  ter, these teeny little robots can fly, crawl, or scurry twice the speed of the fastest human on Earth. Wood hopes that in the future, microro-bots will play a crucial role in search-and-rescue missions, medical breakthroughs, and space exploration. Think of a swarm of thousands of tiny robots going where no man has gone before!

- **LIKE CRUZ'S MOTHER, SCIENTIST ZOLTAN TAKACS** studies how animal venoms may hold the key to treating many human illnesses. Venom  toxins are already used in medicines to treat heart dis-ease and diabetes, and new treatments for autoimmune diseases and cancer could be on the market within a decade. Experts say that with upward of 20 million toxins yet to be screened, we have only scratched the surface of venoms' potential for medicine.

And that's only the beginning! Turn the page for a more complete list of awesome explorers and experts who are paving the way for a better tomorrow.

Real Explorer Inspiration

From conservationists to biologists, anthropologists, and even photographers, National Geographic explorers help us see the world in brand-new ways. Flip back through *The Nebula Secret* and see if you can spot where any of these amazing adventurers might have inspired ideas for Cruz's future world. Then visit exploreracademy.com to read even more explorer biographies and find links to cool content.

MUNAZZA ALAM

ASTRONOMER, UNITED STATES
Munazza Alam uses data from the Hubble Space Telescope to study planets outside the solar system. Her specialty is investigating the atmospheres of these planets and what type of weather exists on these other worlds."

SKYLAR TIBBITS

MATERIALS ARCHITECT, UNITED STATES
Skylar Tibbits's invention of 4-D printing has opened up a world of possibilities for the future of adaptable materials. By creating objects that self-construct, it's possible to create technologies that could be useful anywhere from the emergency room to disaster recovery sites around the world.

TASHI DHENDUP

WILDLIFE BIOLOGIST, BHUTAN Tashi Dhendup is a forestry officer at Bhutan's Department of Forestry and Park Services. He uses camera traps and noninvasive genetics to document endangered species such as tigers and clouded leopards to aid in wild cat conservation.

SANDHYA NARAYANAN

ZOLTAN TAKACS

HERPETOLOGIST/ TOXINOLOGIST, HUNGARY Zoltan Takacs specializes in venomous snakes and snake venoms. He helped to develop a unique method for testing different animal toxins for their potential medicinal use. He also researches coral snakes and cobras to understand why they are immune to their own venom.

LINGUISTIC ANTHROPOLOGIST, PERU Sandhya Narayanan's focus is on understanding how multiple languages are maintained in unique communities around the world, and spreading awareness about how language shapes, and is shaped by, the customs and beliefs of a specific region. She currently works in the Andes, studying the indigenous languages of the area.

ANN DUMALIANG

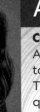

CONSERVATIONIST, THE PHILIPPINES
Ann Dumaliang works to protect steep limestone towers at the Masungi Georeserve in the Philippines. The area is deeply affected by illegal logging and quarrying, and requires protection for both the landforms and wildlife.

GENEVIEVE VON PETZINGER

PALEOANTHROPOLOGIST, CANADA
Genevieve von Petzinger studies cave art from the Ice Age in Europe. She works to record and understand the geometric signs that are found in many of these caves. Having worked at 52 sites across France, Spain, Portugal, and Sicily, she created the first ever database of these mysterious marks and identified relationships between 32 main symbols.

ROBERT WOOD

TECHNOLOGIST, UNITED STATES
Robert Wood is an expert in robots that fly, robots you wear, squishy robots, and teeny-tiny robots the size of a nickel. He leads a team that invents and develops tiny microrobots that may one day play a role in medical care and search-and-rescue missions.

MARTIN WIKELSKI

BEHAVIORAL ECOLOGIST, GERMANY Martin Wikelski is figuring out the mysterious ways that animals—including monarch butterflies—make mass migrations. To understand how they make their massive 3,000-mile (4,830-km) trip, Martin outfitted individual butterflies with tiny radio transmitters to see where they go and how they get there.

BRANWEN WILLIAMS

OCEANOGRAPHER/ENVIRONMENTAL SCIENTIST, UNITED STATES Branwen Williams uses the ocean's coral and algae to record changes in the environment. Focusing on the Pacific and Arctic Oceans, she is able to assess changes in the climate and decipher whether they are due to nature or human activities.

TOPHER WHITE

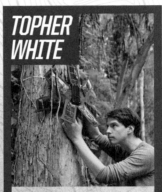

INVENTOR/ ENGINEER, UNITED STATES Topher White has come up with a method of using upcycled smartphones and transforming them into autonomous, solar-powered listening devices that pick up sounds of illegal logging activity and send real-time alerts to local rangers in the forest. Since 2014, Rainforest Connection has protected more than 3.7 million trees.

ANAND VARMA

SCIENCE PHOTOGRAPHER, UNITED STATES
Anand Varma's photographs use special techniques to tell the story behind the science of complex issues. From the secret life cycle of honeybees to the lightning-fast behaviors of hummingbirds, Anand offers a rare glimpse at the world's smallest wonders.

EXPLORER ACADEMY

BOOK 2:
THE FALCON'S FEATHER

51.5074°N   I   0.1278°W

Sailor gave a toaster-size chunk of ice to Bryndis, who handed it off to Cruz, who gently set it on the small pile of rubble near the cave wall. They were trying to clear the exit tunnel. It was painstaking work. The explosion had destabilized the roof of the cave, and every now and then a clump of ice would snap off and hurtle toward them like a frozen missile. They'd have to scurry under the wing of the laughing dragon rock for cover, wait for the dust to settle, then try again. In the past two hours, more new stuff had fallen than they had cleared, but nobody wanted to admit that they were engaged in a pointless mission.

As Sailor reached for another block of ice, a crack echoed through the cavern. *"Run!"* called Cruz.

They made it under the laughing dragon's wing a second before a shower of ice fell on the spot where they'd been standing.

"Great," moaned Sailor. "What are we going to do? We can't go and we can't stay."

"She's right." Bryndis looked at Cruz. "If we keep this up we could trigger another avalanche. But if we don't..."

ACKNOWLEDGMENTS

Writing is a solitary profession, but it doesn't have to be a lonely one, especially if you are blessed with caring friends, family, and colleagues. And I am. Many thanks to my agent, Rosemary Stimola, for her faith in me, along with the occasional pep talk (all in lowercase letters and with assorted emojis).

Thanks to Erica Green, Becky Baines, Jennifer Rees, Eva Absher-Schantz, Scott Plumbe, and the entire National Geographic team for trusting in my vision. You brought joy to the journey, which is every writer's dream. Special thanks to Lisa Owens, the gang at Online Author Visits, and all my SCBWI Western-Washington pals for their support. I'm so very grateful for Debbie Thoma, Marie Thoma, Amber Kizer, Sherry Bells, Bonnie Jackson, Karyn Choo, and all the friends who understood the magnitude of this project and said, "Just keep writing and I'll see you on the other side." As ever, I'm lucky to be supported by an incredible family: my dad, Dean; my father-in-law, Jacques; Jennie; Lori Dru; Dean; Tammy; Austin; Trina; Bailey; and Carter. Now with me in spirit, my mom, Shirley, was my biggest champion and best friend. When I was young, we would always read before I went to sleep, and our favorite books were action-packed tales like *Kidnapped* and *Treasure Island*, and I know she would have enjoyed Cruz's adventures. Finally, thanks to my incredible husband, William, who fills my days with laughter, flowers, and cats!

Cruz's eyes followed the curve of the dragon's wing as it vanished into the blue crystalline ceiling. Daylight was beginning to fade. His body was warm, thanks to his hide-and-seek jacket, but his hands were white with cold. Emmett still had his gloves. Plus, Cruz was starving. There had to be a way out of here. But how?

"Why don't we check Mell's video memory?" suggested Bryndis. "If the weather did affect her analytics, we could be missing a message that someone sent back to us—"

"I already did." Cruz shook his head to indicate there was nothing. "Mell, off."

Two tiny glowing eyes went dark.

Sailor shivered. "Cruz, are you saying…?"

Cruz looked up from the little drone perched on his thumb. "Nobody's coming for us."

Read a longer excerpt from *The Falcon's Feather* at exploreracademy.com.